ELON

JOURNEY TO TRUTH

ISABELLA ADAMS

Foster Embry Publishing, LLC
244 Fifth Avenue, Suite E148
New York, New York 10001
www.fosterembry.com

Printed in the United States of America
First edition, 2019

For Qidira, and all who seek

It is good to have an end to journey towards; but it is the journey itself that matters, in the end.

— URSULA K. LE GUIN

It is when you find yourself alone that you seek out new worlds.

— ANONYMOUS

PROLOGUE

*E*lon." My father beckoned me from where he lay near the fire.

I put my knife down. Rising from the tree trunk that served as my nightly perch, I rested the spear I was making against the worn wood before falling to his side. Kneeling next to the weak old man, the only other living creature on my small island, I grasped his outstretched hand. His fingers were cold and thin. Still, his skin, pale as it was, was darker than mine. In the flickering firelight, I reflected on my mixed genetics, wrestling with familiar confusion about my place in the universe.

I pulled our entwined hands to my chest, hoping I could infuse his cells with my own strength. Tears fell from my eyes as my heart flooded with the certainty that, despite the exceptional longevity granted him by his own heritage, my father would soon leave me forever.

"I'm here," I said.

The reflection of wavering flames danced in his eyes, the once brilliant blue now devoid of his own sparkle. That light disappeared when my mother died the prior year. His heart broke that day and I knew his end was near.

He smiled and the world blossomed once more. "Hoshi, you are my star, my love, my world."

"Then don't leave me," I interrupted. Even though I was over five hundred years old, my adolescent petulance reacted to my father like no other creature in the universe.

He closed his eyes and tears seeped from the corners. They rolled down his pale face to his ears. The prominent brow ridge that defined his people, the Sidar, stuck out through his gray skin more than it had before. It had been a while since fat stood between his thin dermis and his delicate bones, and his skull was no exception.

"I mean," I started, unable to avoid my own attempt at levity, "I could try to enhance my mind-control powers and take over some of the humans so I won't be alone. I could create my own army of Elonionites, but I don't think that's what you had in mind for my future."

He laughed. The effort cost him and he had to wait for a wave of coughs to subside before continuing. Reaching up, he patted my cheek. "Never lose your sense of humor."

I heard his voice in my head. *"It is time, Hoshi."*

"No," I whispered out loud. I closed my eyes and held his hand against my cheek. Try as I might to suppress them, my shoulders shook as I gave into waiting sobs. All humor was gone; there was no hope left in my heart.

"Do not cry, my love. Take solace in the knowledge that I will be with your mother soon. And I know she is so very proud of you." His voice caressed my mind like a summer breeze. The warmth was bittersweet, however. For with the comfort of his thoughts came painful memories of my mother's passing. In an effort to run from my excruciating sense of emotional implosion, I retreated to memories of happier times, before my mother died.

I was born on my parents' home planet of Sidra. When I arrived, my thick, gray skin betrayed my mother's partial river troll DNA. Within a few years, even our own community questioned her fitness to be a mother. Their fear of her long-held-secret genetics trumped all past experience with those of mixed heritage. Worried for our safety, concerned that some well-meaning Sidar would separate us, my parents fled the only home they had known, hoping to keep me safe.

"We are Other," my mother told me as we rocketed through the darkness toward an unknown future. "Sidra is safe for Other, normally, but . . ." She never told me more than that and I never asked. I thought she would tell me more when she was ready.

That never happened, though. Once we settled on our new planet, she instead set about teaching me everything she knew about science, astrology, literature, and the religions of the universe. When I was not busy with my studies, my mother regaled me with stories about dwarfs, fairies, and epic battles. Her ability to create happiness despite hardship was boundless and we never had time to dwell on the negative aspects of our past.

She told me stories about her childhood as well. My grandmother, one of the few fully genetic humans on Sidra, was attacked by a river troll and the resulting pregnancy ended in her banishment from her closed human community. She went to a nearby Sidar city and found work. When my mother was born, pale and beautiful, she looked human, and my grandmother breathed with relief. As my mother grew, her strength belied her troll genetics, and my grandmother knew, despite being a unique Other, my mother would survive.

As she aged, my mother's thick, blonde hair aided her acceptance by the Sidar. Her pale skin was similar as well, yet the slight iridescence with which it shimmered in the sun made her an oddity.

My father was also born on Sidra, to a Sidar father and a vamphyre mother. On Sidra, the two races had a tumultuous past, but still, they shared the planet. This tenuous peace, however, meant they rarely intermarried, making my father a curiosity among his peers.

"When I met your mother," my father used to say, "I fell so in love I swore she was a siren. I cared little of what anyone said or any warnings about staying away from humans."

My mother would blush and look at my father from the corner of her misty blue eyes, which shifted like the sea. "What is meant to be will be," she would say. "Besides, how could any woman—vamphyre, Sidar, human, or Other—resist you?"

When my mother died, my father stopped eating. While I am not pure Sidar, I still have the empathic connection. My heart broke with his that day, and I felt him lose his will to live.

Now, sitting in the dark on our chosen planet, my father's voice sounded in my brain again. "*Elon.*"

Hearing him in my mind calmed me and my tears slowed. I wiped my face with my free hand, and then, in the low light of the lingering flames, I gazed at my long, gray fingers until my father interrupted my musings once more.

"*We have prepared you well,*" he relayed. "*You are ready. Never doubt your ability.*" Without thought, I responded with telepathic resistance. His assertion of my aptitude meant only one thing: he was at peace with leaving me alone. I, however, was far from ready to accept his departure.

He continued, interrupting my opposition, "*There is no one like you anywhere in the universe. In no galaxy will you find someone who shares your beauty, strength, and destiny. Never forget what we have taught you: your gifts are unique to you; you can use them to serve yourself or you can serve others. The choice is yours. Choose wisely."*

I touched his face and my hands trembled with grief. He smiled.

"Stay here, if you must," he continued, *"but do not stay just to mourn us. Go, as we have prepared you to do. Your service to life will be strong, and wherever you are, wherever you go, we will be with you. So, go into the universe and find where you are meant to be. Remember, though, never underestimate yourself, or your enemy."*

His grasp slackened. I felt his spirit dissipate into the universe and loneliness unlike I had ever experienced crushed me into the cold earth.

"No!" I howled.

I threw myself over his lifeless body, sure that my voice carried across the water to the mainland, where scattered human settlements existed in caves. I knew they thought of us as monsters. Sometimes they set out offerings of food, no doubt hoping we would leave them alone. I couldn't blame them. Every now and then a vamphyre ship descended in a thunder of fire and wind, and the invaders feasted on the primitive human population. How were the humans to know I was not like the other vamphyres?

On that warm, moonless night, however, I did not care. The weight of my solitude enveloped me. My thick skin, which, thanks to my mother's genetics, was nearly impenetrable, felt like it would split open from my pain. My thoughts flew from my head, searching for some connection. I touched a few scared human minds, verifying my hunch that my scream had reached their ears, but I could not find another familiar soul. I stretched my mind as far as it would go; I ran from my body, fleeing the sadness that consumed me. I traveled the planet we called Terra until I exhausted all of my energy and fell, spent and defeated, into a crumpled heap next to the fire.

The next morning, I buried my father on the bluff next to my mother. I gathered my few belongings, my precious books of language, music, and science. I cleared away a year's worth of unattended underbrush and climbed into the ship we arrived in all those years ago. Tears stung my eyes. My parents' teachings on how to use the technology burned in my mind, having recited it back to them every year on my birthday for centuries. Still, I didn't care. I had no desire to return to Sidra, or to any other known planet.

I had no family. I was alone.

At that moment, grief-stricken and raw, I wanted nothing more than to jettison from this lonely planet and die amongst the stars.

ELON

*Y*ou . . .are such . . .a pain in the ass." I stood over a wounded vamphyre, trying to catch my breath. As she recovered from our most recent tussle, which had sent her sprawling into the murky marsh waters, I pressed my foot against her throat. I was too tired to fight her again.

Straw-like strands of blonde hair escaped my braid and fell into my eyes. With a sigh, I wiped them out of my face. The vamphyre upon whom my foot rested hissed and spat at me. Her continued attitude only annoyed me so I bent over and ruefully shoved her head underwater, watching my fingers as they shimmered beneath the brackish, boggy puddle. The image of my fingers splayed wide across her face, gray and strong, pulled the memory of my father's death from deep in my gut. Sorrow would not help my current errand, so I banished my sadness back to the dark corners of my mind.

My victim's hair waved around her thin, angry face like black seagrass. While I knew that as a full-blooded vamphyre she could not drown, I still enjoyed watching her glare at me from beneath the water while her legs flailed and her claws gouged unsuccessfully at my arm. I considered her dark eyes as I deliberated on what mode of execution I should use: a stake through the heart, sunlight, fire, decapitation, or exsanguination. Nothing else would ensure her permanent demise.

I began tracking this vamphyre early the prior evening. I started in the forest to the west, where the vamphyres live. She was easy to find; most rogue vamphyres are, as they often leave a trail of destruction behind them. She fought back, and here we were in the pre-dawn light, in the marsh that made up most of Palus, the planet I had called home for the last ten turns around the sun.

To the north were the gray mountains, to the west was the forest. The sea dominated both the southern and eastern edges of the wetlands in which I lived. So, whenever it was time to seek out an unstable vamphyre, I always started in the forest. No vamphyres ventured into the mountains, not if they wanted to live to tell their story. No one knew why, but any Palusian vamphyre who did attempt a journey into the snowy hills, was never heard from again.

As a rule, I dislike going after vamphyres, but this female had gotten night-sick. Too many years of no sunlight coupled with too many small, dark spaces robbed her of her sense of community and she began feeding on some of the human inhabitants who lived at the base of the mountains.

There are only two settlements of humans on this planet, but there are also vamphyres and, deep in the mountains, Sidar. That's why when I landed here, I stayed. I felt their pull, but while it was comforting to know they were near, I never went to them. Most of the humans lived in the settlement at the base of the mountains. Some, however, had moved into caves to the east, near the water. They felt safer there, less like food for what lives in the forest. And while I know that the humans are scared of me, they still trust me. I figure it is because I look mostly human, and humans seem less scared of things similar to themselves.

I thought back to the conversation that triggered last night's particular hunt. I recalled the words spoken by one of the village elders as we sat in the town hall.

"You must find this vile creature and deal with it," he had said.

I attempted to keep my face neutral but failed. My annoyance with his declaration that vamphyres were "creatures" crept into my tone. "Vamphyres are not all bad, you know."

His eyes narrowed. "They cannot be trusted."

Ignoring the obvious irony of the moment, I shrugged. "It's true that they mostly look out for their own, but the sects are solitary. You can't lump this particular blood-sucker in with the rest of the vamphyre population. It's not fair."

I knew it was useless. Too many times I had attempted to correct their misconceptions and too many times they continued to ignore logic. I mentally reviewed my usual lecture: the behavior of a vamphyre is dictated by many factors, as it is in all other genetic groups. It also makes a difference if one is born with the altered genetics, as I was, or became vamphyric by *acquiring* the virus. For some reason, the acquired virus interacts poorly with already established genetic codes and causes more aberrant behavior.

When I give this well-rehearsed speech, I often receive a comment about how all vamphyres should be locked away to avoid contaminating "normal people." I remind those listening that the virus is transmitted via bodily fluids and is not contagious through casual contact, reminding them, once again, that being a vamphyre is not abnormal, just different.

Still, I couldn't blame the townspeople for their fear. They had, after all, lost loved ones to some of the night-sick vamphyres. They watched the virus take hold, which happened anywhere from a few days to a few months after infection. The time it took for changes to occur—light sensitivity, elongated canine teeth, inability to create hemoglobin to carry oxygen—depended on the host's individual DNA. Soon, however, the repair mechanisms of the infected individual's body became nearly flawless. Yet despite this newly acquired ability to regenerate, they lost the ability to be out during daylight. In addition, an occasional blood meal became necessary for their survival. Other than that, though, they could live forever.

I stared at the elder and rubbed my eyes to hide my frustration. "More vamps have been aggressive lately, that's true."

Something was indeed happening with the vamphyre population. Some killed themselves in daylight. Others lived through the day in the darkest part of the woods, accepting the burns they encountered when leaves shifted and sunlight touched them. Whatever it was, though, this change in the planet's vamphyres felt big, and inevitable.

Now, standing over my night's prey, my irritation with what she put me through turned to sadness. I cursed my human emotions and watched as some of the precious blood she had stolen leaked from her wounds, wounds I had inflicted. The crimson liquid mingled with brackish water, swirling and exposing the small current that ran through the marsh on its way to open water.

I followed the small stream with my eyes and eventually

rested my gaze on the Palusian sea. The vamphyre under me struggled, but I merely leaned harder against her neck and she calmed down once more.

The wind from the mountains promised a cool day and carried the crisp smell of snow. The sky was a palate of blues and grays, bleeding to yellows and oranges over the water where the sun was rising. I lifted my hand and my adversary's head came out of the water.

It took her but a moment to notice the sun cresting the horizon, and soon panic took hold. She scratched at my leg, which still held her down. She kicked out with all of her strength, trying in vain to free herself so she could outrun the sunrise. All of her anger was gone, though. She fought with the feral effort of a trapped animal.

"I'm sorry," I said. And I was.

The first fingers of sunlight burst over the horizon, and I removed my foot from her neck. She scrambled to hide behind one of the mounds of grass and dirt that defined this area as marsh, but it was too late. Her attempt to shield her face failed and soon her arms burned away. She screamed as her hair caught on fire. The flames wasted no time in consuming her entire body. She burned down to the water, and all that was left were two disembodied legs. The stray limbs flopped forward and floated to the surface. When the sun rose higher that patch would boil as the flesh burned.

I turned my face back to the sun, hands on my hips. Tears escaped my eyes and burned salty trails down my cheeks. I hated knowing I was the last person she would ever see, that I was the last thing she would either plead with or curse.

I did things like this because I was stronger than the humans, because my skin was thicker and the fibers of my muscles were more durable. I fought for them because I could track the vamphyres and because they could not hurt me as they could a human. I could withstand a bite or two, and if the attacker's teeth succeeded in breaking my skin, the virus would not attack my blood the same as it would others. I did things like this because others on this planet could not. *"Your gifts are unique to you; you can use them to serve yourself or you can serve others. The choice is yours. Choose wisely,"* my father had said.

Through my tears I whispered into the new dawn, "I'm trying, Papa."

QIDIRA

I tried to dry my tears on the arm of my already wet shirt and I realized how tired I was. With one last look at what was left of my night's objective, I set off toward the mountains, and toward my home. After a few steps, I saw the small figure of Qidira running toward me. She sped over the grass and soil, and then tried to run through the water, which only slowed her progress. Her fluid cursing floated through the morning mist.

She made me smile. I put up my hand to signal her to stop where she was. She did not listen, which did not surprise me because she never did. Her long black hair was pulled away from her face into a clip at the top of her head and the rest of it flowed down her back. Her skirts were sodden and muddy, but she continued to mutter to herself —and to the water, I think—as she plowed through another muddy pool.

When I got closer, I yelled, "Wait, you stubborn little dwarf."

She threw up her hands, huffed, and said, "I have *been* waiting."

"Obstinate woman," I said under my breath, but still I hovered over the uneven terrain to hasten my movement.

Flying always takes a lot of energy, more than I thought I had at that moment, but I knew there was a full meal waiting for me when I got home, so I used what I had left. Besides, I was scared Qidira would trip on something and fall face first into the water. Then I would have to calm her as she threatened to dry up every drop of water on this planet; and *then* I would have to listen as she apologized to the Gods and vocalized her acceptance that things were as they should be and that she was sorry she was so willful, and on and on. As I reached the mound upon which she stood, she threw her solid four-foot one-inch frame at me and wrapped her graceful arms around my neck.

"Thank you, thank you, thank you," she cried.

"For what, for what, for what?"

"For not dying and for killing that awfully scary bloodsucker. Not that I was scared . . ."

"Here, hop on, I'll carry you home." I shouldered my bag and Qidira allowed me to shift her to my back. Together, we set off toward our house on the edge of town.

Qidira was Other as well: half-dwarf, part human, and part something else that neither of us could identify. She was difficult to get along with for some, which was why we were friends. I was used to solitude and quiet, and living with Qidira was a good balance for me. Plus, she cooked and cleaned, and I, well, I did not.

While the nearby village was inhabited mostly by humans, there were a few Other there. Some distant Sidar human mixes and a few diluted vamphyre mixes, but nothing too threatening to the rest of the people. Qidira was one of the few dwarfs I had ever met, and the only one in our town. She obviously inherited the height of her dwarf parent, but it was easy to see that her personality was not all genetic. She was ornery and protective like the dwarfs, but the strength of will was all her own.

In the distance, I saw the settlement beyond our house. All of the structures were made out of wood, built on stilts to avoid the inevitable wet that occurred when it rained and the marsh became swollen. I shifted my eyes back to our home, which stood past the edge of town. It was the only domain that lived in the heart of the marsh, and it loomed, strong and solid, between where I now carried Qidira and the rest of the homes. I was, once again, struck by how beautiful it was. Qidira had built it when she arrived in the settlement and her elegant touch adorned every inch.

Visible from this distance were the sun carving at one end of the peaked roof and the moon at the other. Between them, crafted representations of Gods from various cultures and religions throughout the galaxy decorated the soaring spine of the house. Qidira was a strong believer that there were Gods out there. She also knew she would not truly know who they were until she died, so she was not taking any chances. She placed the wooden figures on the roof for protection. She prayed to them all daily, and often when she muttered to herself, I knew she was sending her thoughts and prayers up through the ceiling.

We reached the base of our home as the sun cleared the horizon. A short but elegant staircase made of hardwood from the forest led to a porch which ran around the entire structure. When she built them, Qidira had carved the railings into chains of shells and waves, etching waving grass into the front of the stairs themselves.

On the porch, two hammocks hung limp among potted plants that were surrounded by a smattering of fishing supplies. Shells and scraps of wood lay along the railing, peaceful reminders of prior outings. A driftwood wind chime dangled from one corner, and a large iridescent shell hung over the front door.

Fresh herbs grew in planters that hung over the porch railings. Scraps of greenery on the wooden floor remained as evidence of Qidira's recent harvest. As we climbed the stairs, I also saw where she had killed and cleaned a fish, and then tried to wash away the blood. Whatever she had prepared on the weather-worn slatted wood was now cooking inside, its savory smell inviting me home.

Qidira moved past me and through the open door. Judging by the multiple mugs and dirty plates scattered along the top step, I assumed she had watched the end of the fight. Both vamphyres and dwarfs have amazing night vision and I was sure this helped assuage her feelings of powerlessness, which was a common angst for her while I was out hunting. I followed her into our home, breathing in the comforting smell of jasmine and breakfast.

The house was in essence one, large open space. The front two thirds reached up to the peaked roof and a loft overhung the back third of the room. On the left side of the space, towards the back, curved stairs led to the elevated area, which was not walled off but instead was protected by a railing that ran from the stairs to the opposite wall. The sense of openness was healing.

Large windows dominated the walls of the entire structure, and two circular windows sat at the top of the front and back walls, near the apex of the roof. A door on the back wall opened to the back porch. There, a ladder led down to the wooden walkway that connected us to the town.

As I walked in, I noticed that Qidira had run me a bath. The steaming metal tub waited next to our wood burning stove, whose chimney pipe soared up the western wall and disappeared through the roof.

"Go wash and then come eat," Qidira said as she moved toward the kitchen area on the right. She began taking food from the cooking stove to the table, which sat on a platform by the front door.

I dragged myself over to the tub and gratefully stripped off my cold, wet clothes. I left them on the stone slabs next to the hot metal where they hissed as steam rose from the damp material. As I sank into the delicious water, I got a nose full of lavender and something else.

Comfrey.

Qidira had added some, assuming I would be sore when I returned. Gratitude for her washed over me as I laid my head back against the tub, hung my hands over the side, and drifted into a light sleep.

HOME

*W*hite faces swam in and out of focus in my head. Voices called my name and I felt the safety of the Sidar surrounding me. One face, someone I had seen before but did not know, solidified. Yellow hair hung around his aged features. When he spoke, his voice held fear I had heretofore never heard from a Sidar, not even my father. "We need you. . . please help."

My eyes flew open as, in my half-awake state, something touched my arm. I grabbed whatever it was, sending water flying all over the floor, and all over Qidira. She put her hand over mine.

"Come eat," she said gently. She pulled both of her hands free and brushed sudsy bath remnants from her newly changed skirts. "I let you sleep for a while, but it is time to eat."

She picked up a blanket from the stool next to the tub and held it open for me. With some retaliation from my sore muscles, I climbed out of the bath and wrapped myself in the woven softness. I padded over to the table, still feeling the warmth of my dream.

But was it a dream? This time seemed so real.

The Sidar often came to me in my sleep; it was part of our nature. But they had never spoken to me before. Usually, I just heard my name and felt their love and acceptance. Ruminating on this change of behavior, I sat down at the table and took a deep breath. I drank in the scent of warm, crispy fish, herbs, cooked roots, and moist sweet bread.

"This looks amazing. I would starve without you, really I would," I said as I tied the blanket in a knot under my arm.

"I know," Qidira said as she served the food.

I poured golden grape juice into goblets and placed one in front of her. Fresh water was easy to find in the center of the village where a river ran down from the mountains and into the marsh, but Marsh Grapes were harder to come by. We were lucky, however. The sweet fruit grew all over the base of our house, so we always had the straw-colored juice at meals. When we both had food and drink in front of us, we clasped our hands in front of our chests and bowed our heads. Together, we offered a simple prayer of thanksgiving for the food.

"Itadakimasu."

Qidira let me eat a few bites before she asked questions. I told her about going into the forest, to the vamphyre settlement of Grod Mesto; about finding the sect leader, waiting with them through their meal of forest animal, and the grape juice I brought as an offering. I did not tell her I had eaten some of the raw meat with them. The vamphyre in me still craved fresh blood every now and then, but Qidira never liked to hear that part. The meal had served a dual purpose. Not only did it fortify me for the ensuing fight, but eating with them showed that, while I may be Other, I am still part vamphyre.

They had shared with me their knowledge of the area in which the rogue female was living and they sent two scouts with me most of the way. Qidira was done eating when I got to the part about finding my target screaming, covered in the blood of something undisclosed. I recounted her initial attack but then breezed over the blow-by-blow, hitting the highlights.

The vamphyre had rushed at me from the shadows, knocking me against a tree. I reached up and grabbed a low branch. In an attempt to gain leverage, I pulled myself up and into the tree, but she flew up to meet me. With nothing to lose, she dove for my neck.

I was able to deflect her, but still, her bloody canines landed against my shoulder. Unable to satisfy her yearning for flesh, she howled in frustration at how tough my skin was and I was able to get her by the throat. My arms were longer than hers, so I held her away from me as I floated back down to the ground and over to my bag. I bound her hands with tough cord, which proved difficult. She, of course, did not want to acquiesce and I ended up holding her down by sitting on her chest in order to complete my knot. Eventually, I started walking her out toward the marsh. While I had wooden stakes and a large knife with me, I had decided to let the rising sun deliver the final blow.

We had a lot of ground to cover and as I dragged her along, she fought me. At one point she kicked my knees out from under me and ran. I found the ropes a short distance away but could not find her. I knew that if I kept going, *she* would find *me*, so I just kept walking. Sure enough, in a few short moments, she jumped out of a tree and on top of me. Her blows to my face and body were vicious, which explained the discoloration blooming over my cheek and forehead. In the end, I got her under control and marched her out into the open. Again, she got loose and ran, not toward the forest, but toward the sea. She screeched as she went, a high-pitched cry that dripped with insanity and desperation. After an energy-expensive chase, I caught her once more, and Qidira had seen the rest.

"Did you lose your knife again? I expect you will want me to make you another one." Her voice held the pretense of annoyance and barely hid the vestiges of her worry. She continued to grumble as she cleared the table.

"No, Qid, I did not, I have it with my gear, thank you very much."

"Whatever." She pouted, with her back to me. Her shoulders rose as she took a breath, and when she spoke again, it was with an air of defeat. "Whatever."

I loved Qidira. She was like a part of me I had not known was missing. Sometimes, however, I wanted to poke her in her small dwarfish eyes.

I got up from the table and carried the last of the food to the kitchen. Qidira opened the trap door in the floor that led down to our cold-storage box. I handed her the bowl of sweet bread and, as she placed the dish on a shelf, she half disappeared into the metal container that hung from the underside of our house.

When she reemerged, I said, "I'm going to sleep some more." I helped her close the trap door and gave her a hug. "Thank you so much for the food."

Craving more sleep, I moved toward the stairs. The muscles in my shoulders and back ached where I strained them in the fight. I was also beginning to feel where the vamphyre slammed me into the ground. My backside was sure to be bruised later.

Halfway up the stairs, a large ornately etched looking glass hung on the wall. I stopped as I glimpsed my reflection. My long, yellow hair hung wet around my face and spilled down my chest like woven silk thread. I tossed my head to move it all behind my shoulders but stopped mid-motion because of pain. I winced as I waited for the pounding to subside, and when the throbbing stopped, I opened my eyes and relaxed my shoulders.

Squaring my torso in front of the mirror, I used my hands to gather my hair and hang it down my back. It fell below my shoulder blades and I thought, *I need to cut that.* I noticed that my left shoulder was swollen, and it would have looked more purplish had it not been for the silvery tint of my skin. I could see where the vamphyre had scratched me with her canines. She had actually broken the first few layers of my thick dermis.

Impressive, I mused.

As far as I could see, I was only bleeding from a couple of spots: a gash on my right forearm, which I had sustained during the struggle on the forest floor, and a split in my bottom lip, delivered by a swift knee to the face. Thanks to my vamphyre DNA, however, I was already healing.

I lifted my hands to my face and inspected them. I had broken a nail. I remembered it happened as I was trying to tie up the struggling vamphyre. Vamphyres are strong and it had taken a good amount of my strength to get her under control. My eyes focused back on my reflection and I noticed that the left side of my face was swollen, too.

A dark bruise ran from my broad forehead to my small, pointed chin. My cheekbones were noticeable on my trian-gle-shaped face, and as I touched my left cheek, I thought the skin would split due to the pressure of the growing hematoma. My tongue played out of the right side of my mouth and licked at the now healing wound on my lower lip. While the rest of my skin was abnormally thick due to my troll heritage, my lips were human—red and tender, and easy to break. *Still, vamp parentage heals it all,* I thought as I took in a long, deep breath.

I stared into my own round blue eyes and saw my mother. Suddenly, my heart ached for my parents, and I moved from simply feeling tired to being a passel of emotion. I forced myself to stand still, staring at my reflection. I had to allow my full feelings to wash through me. It was the only way they would pass.

And pass they did, like a steady, boiling stream. Sadness, longing, loss, anger, loneliness, joy, and back to loss again. Soon, my heart swelled and the tears came. As they fell, I watched myself cry for everything I had lost, everyone I loved, and everything I had done. Soon, the stream moved along and I was once again back to being grateful for Qidira, home, food, and sleep. I thanked the Gods and smiled.

When I reached the carpeted upstairs, I took great joy in feeling the rich, woven rug between my toes. The floor coverings were made in dwarfish tradition out of elements that no one should be able to create into textiles. *Whatever she does*, I thought, *is cool.*

The loft area had no walls. Instead, it was separated by silk screens we had made together, with pictures from where both of us grew up. We each had our own sleeping area set on opposite sides of the space and in the middle, under the large, round window, lived a low altar carved with delicate birds, suns, flowers, animals, water, and stars. On the small table sat a perfectly round bluish-gray stone supported by driftwood. The stone was so smooth I often ran my hand over and over it during meditation. It had a calming effect and soothed even my most ragged emotions. Dried sage and heather lay in front of the stone, waiting to be burned during moments of reflection. To the left was a small bowl of sand that held remnants of old offerings, and colorful pillows littered the floor.

Our separate living areas were distinct to our personalities—I had dark curtains over all of the windows, with my white lavender-stuffed mattress resting on a simple platform of wood in the middle of the wall. Qidira had made me an elegant set of shelves where I folded my clothes and kept the books and other personal items that had made it with me this far.

Qidira's space was dominated by a majestic bed, with posts at all corners that supported rails between them. The wood was carved in twists, with bursts of lines swirling around the supports. Hung from the rails were thin, light-colored silk curtains, which were pulled back to the headboard with gold velvet ribbon. Her mattress was thick, stuffed with cloth and heather. She kept red spray roses on either side of her bed, and she had a magnificent armoire against the side wall. The floor was covered with an intricate rug, woven from I did not know what.

I stopped by the altar and tried to sit, but my muscles retaliated once again.

I bowed my head and thought, *Thank you Gods . . . for survival, for Qidira, for home and food. And thanks for my bed. I love my bed.* I deepened the bow, a motion that elicited a moan as I felt the ache in my back. Still, I maintained my bend long enough to run my hand over the stone.

Once in my room, I changed into a long, soft shirt and climbed under my covers. Qidira had set flowers on my bedside table—fragile morning glories in a round, hand blown glass vase. The blues and purples made me smile as I closed my eyes.

THE SIDAR

*I*t did not take long before I felt the Sidar, and soon I saw the same face that had come to me in the tub. Only this time, instead of seeing him in my head, I felt my bare feet standing on a stone floor.

Soon, the area around me became clearer and I found myself in a dark space with a rocky ceiling and walls. The only light came from a fire in the middle of the cave. Shadows flickered into the blackness of three corridors, which led away from the mysterious nook, this secret cavern in which the Sidar hid. Attempting to move, I backed into the cave wall. I stayed, pressed against the rough stone as I looked out at the men and women sitting around on the floor.

They were all dressed in flowing cloth. Their identical white skin shone in the wavering darkness and the prominent facial ridge that curved from above the eyebrows down to the lower jaw cast shadows over their eyes. They all had thick, yellow-blonde hair that fell down their backs. Every one of them had their eyes closed. Standing in front of me was the man I had seen earlier. His features were more defined this time and I saw that he was older than most of the others in the room. Unlike the others, however, his eyes were open and looking right into mine.

"Elon, thank you for allowing us to bring you here." His voice was rough like an old man, and yet it flowed through my head like warm milk. With a smile, he raised his hands, fingers up, palms facing me. I hesitated but matched my hands to his. In an instant, I felt his feelings. His wisdom and need sped through my entire body. When it reached my toes, I staggered, but did not pull away.

His lips did not move, but his voice sounded in my head. *"We have never truly met. I am Emir, the elder of this Sidar sect. I have watched over you since you arrived, always sending you our invitation to join us. We value your ability to choose and have waited for you to come to us, but we cannot wait any longer. We need your help. We do not belong here, on this planet. We do not belong in these caves, but we have stayed for generations protecting the Star.*

"This is where the true Sidra is, Elon. That is the reason you ended up here—it was not pure chance; it was the Star, it pulled you here. The others are still living on our ancestral planet of Sidra, but years ago the Star was moved here. That was before the vamphyres and before the humans. When we arrived, we made an agreement with the dwarfs." My eyes widened and I opened my mouth to speak, but he continued, *"Yes, there are dwarfs here, ancient dwarfs that live in and under these mountains. Elon, we must protect the Star. Please help."*

Again, I felt his need, and it frightened me. His face became fuzzy, and the feeling of his hands against mine faded. I reached out to touch him, but I was already being pulled through swirling fog. When I opened my eyes, I was in my bed.

I must have been asleep for a while because it was dark. The only illumination came from the moon, and a shaft of silver light streaked across my room. I heard the noises of the marsh at night, but other than that, the house was quiet; Qidira must have been asleep. I threw back the covers and, ignoring the rebellion from my muscles, ran down the stairs to the back porch. I stood against the rail in the cold night air, straining to see anything other than the silhouette of the mountains against the blue night sky. Thunder rumbled in the distance and I shuddered. Clasping my arms tight around my body, I knew that someday soon I would know what was on the other side of those hills.

TEA AND GRAPES

I slept fitfully for the rest of the night, finally getting out of bed when the sun rose. It was raining and Qidira had started a fire in the wood stove. I put on pants, pulled back my hair with twine, and went downstairs. Qidira was sitting in the middle of the floor working on a large piece of cloth. I recognized it as something she was making for the town's medicine person.

She had been working on it for weeks—weaving parts of it, and then embroidering elaborate decorations amidst the entwined fibers. The shaman occasionally stopped by to give direction, and I could tell that if he gave one more "point of clarification," Qidira would weave a dwarfish curse into it somewhere. The composition was elaborate, with constellations, waves, fish, and runic symbols. She had found some precious lapis and somehow spun it into thread. She was now working it around the edges of the cloth in an intricate design. Dwarfs have a way with stone that none of the rest of us will ever be able to master. Qidira never did it in front of me, not because I think she was trying to hide anything, but because I think it took a lot out of her and she could not concentrate when someone else was there.

I went into the kitchen and opened the trap door. Retrieving the sweet bread from the night before and a small pitcher of cream, I joined her on the floor.

"Want some?" I asked.

"I ate, thank you," she replied. "I also made Bebi Tea. It's on the stove."

"Thanks."

I got up, found a stone mug, and poured myself some of the strong concoction Qidira made from a marsh plant. It was sweet and musty, and it always left me feeling stronger than normal. I dumped ample amounts of cane juice in and added all the cream the mug could hold.

"Why the Bebi today, Qid?"

"I thought you could use it." She did not look up from her work.

"Are you approaching a deadline? Why are you up so early?" I took a gulp of tea and sputtered as it burned my throat. I chased the steaming liquid with a bite of sweet bread, hoping to soothe the sting.

"The rain woke me. And I had other things to finish before I got to this. Besides, the sooner this is out of my house the better." She held it at arm's length to look at her work.

"It's beautiful." I took another bite of bread and managed to continue, through a mouthful of moist crumbs, "Can we keep it?"

She snorted. "I do not want this thing here. Not after all the drama it has caused. No, I will make you your own, if you want one." It was some kind of protective, spiritual blanket tapestry thing. I knew how much of herself Qidira was putting into it and I knew what it would mean to her to make one for the house.

"Okay," I said. "I would offer to help but . . ." I laughed.

I was not bad at sewing, but it was piece work I was good at. Qidira made the cloth, wove it, and imbibed it with her magic. These parts of her talent always lead me to think she was part fairy. She did amazing things with single reams of mountain wool and silk. She would make our clothes sometimes, but it was me who sewed the pieces together, especially if there was any leather involved. But I was laughing not because I thought I could not help, but because the thought of me sitting in one place for any amount of time was just funny. She must have thought so too, because she let out a deep chuckle.

"You just make me my new boots and we will call it even." She looked up and smiled.

I stood up and stared out of the window toward the marsh and the ocean. I repeated the same thought I had been having all night: *what was this Star, the Sidra?* My parents had never told me about it. The only Sidra I knew was the planet of my birth.

As I went over and over the events of the prior evening in my mind, I tried to remember anything that might lead me back to the dark cave. I could not recall any defining characteristics that would act as a trail. Perhaps I would have to wait for them to come to me again. Soon, I sensed someone near me, no, inside of me . . . fog rolled in front of my eyes. . . white faces appeared. . .

"Hello?" Qidira was standing next to me, her hand on my shoulder. "Your eyes shifted, Elon." She looked at me, apprehension coloring her face. "I have never seen you do that before. What is going on?" I realized that my hand was halfway to my mouth with a fork full of food.

"I don't know."

I told her about my dream in the tub, and then about

the visitation last night—about what they told me about the dwarfs, and about this thing, this Star; and I told her what I had just seen and felt. "I've never had the connection when I've been awake before."

As a rule, I could always sense when a Sidar was nearby, but until now it had been an intuitive feeling, a sense in my gut, but never while I was awake had I had the connection I just experienced.

She pulled me to the table. Once seated, she kept her eyes trained toward the ground.

"There are other dwarfs here," Qidira said. It was a statement, not a question. "That's how the Sidar here do it . . . that's what I was sent for." Her voice dropped to the tone she used when she talked to herself. I could tell she was seeing her past, thinking about the man she loved, and about her son, who was somewhere in the mountains. About dwarfs, stonework, and magic.

"I've never seen them," I said. "In all of my time here with you, in all of my travels in the forest . . . you'd think I would have run into at least one."

"No, not if they didn't want to be seen or found. Dwarfs are tricky like that. They also prefer to stay in the mountains, and you have never been in the mountains, have you?"

"I've been to the first settlement up the river—or what's left of it . . ." I stopped there. We did not talk about the mountains much, especially not about when Qidira had lived in them. But she knew the settlement I was speaking of—she had lived there as she made her way down to the village after her sweetheart left her. She and her son had weathered a storm in that small settlement. All she had said about it was that there were a lot of Other there; that most of the Other who used to live down here in the marshes moved up there, where they stayed until one day everyone disappeared.

Qidira arrived on this planet as part of a trade mission. She had been sent to negotiate with the Sidar people for precious metals. She and her counterpart negotiator, Amil, had fallen in love, and when her ship left, she stayed behind. Not long after that, they had a baby, a boy, who they named Tariq. Together they lived with a group of mixed Sidar Other on the rise of the mountains, but soon Amil could not ignore the connection to his people. He left her and the boy and went deep into the hills.

Qidira waited for him, until the boy was two years old. Unable to continue feeding her son, she moved down into the marsh, down to the settlement at the bottom of the mountains. She built the house we now lived in, and many others throughout the village. When Tariq was old enough to choose, he, too, left to be with the Sidar. Qidira stayed here, waiting for them both to return. She had never gone after them nor had she asked me to find them. And I had never offered.

"It's okay, Elon. Yes, I forgot that you went up there."

No one knows what happened in that first town up the river. One day there was a settlement of Other there, bringing down metals, stone, and animals for trade, and then there was nothing. The people had sent me up to investigate and I found no one. A couple of homes looked like there had been a struggle, and some looked as if the inhabitants had meant to leave. There were houses with everything still in them, dinner rotting on the table. And there were domesticated animals foraging around for food. I brought back all of the precious materials I could find— fur, leather, metals, and stones. I had not found a single person or even any bodies. There was just no one. Trappers and hunters used that settlement now as their base camp when they ventured into the hills, but no one dared go by themselves, and no one stayed for long. Magic was not common among humans, but superstitions ran deep.

Qidira reached over and touched my fading bruise. "Oh, honey. That looks like it hurts." Her features contorted with sympathy.

"Yes, it does." The cut on my arm was all but gone, and while my lip had healed, there was still a beautiful bruise to mark the spot.

"How about you go pick some grapes and I will make you something for it," she said.

I stood up slowly, still stiff from injury and now from my moments of inactivity. "Ugg. Give me a moment to change."

I went upstairs and changed into wading pants and a short-sleeved shirt. I braided my hair down my back and then tied the braid in a knot. By the time I made it back downstairs, the morning's rain had stopped and slivers of sun shot through the clouds, sending spotlights into the distance. Qidira handed me a wooden bowl on my way out of the door, and I trotted down the front stairs, into the bog.

The water of the marsh changed based on where one stood and on how much rain there had been. Because of the rain, the marsh was swollen, so there was less grass to walk on around the house. It also meant I was unable to see to the bottom of the standing pools.

I stepped into the water, careful to avoid anything swimming toward the sea, and waded to the first piling under the house. White grapes grew up around the wood, the fruit glistening with moisture. The vine continued along the underside of the house, leaving a bountiful, hanging garden. Closer to the forest blue grapes grew on anything they could cling to, but we were lucky to have our own crop of the paler fruit year-round just under our home.

I worked my way around one side of the house, avoiding pools of water that looked too grimy. Only once did I feel something swim past my leg. My brain allowed me to believe it was something simply passing through, not something that normally resided amidst the silt and debris. There were few creatures that could live in these marshy waters, and those that could were either too small to worry about, or so nasty that I did not want to mess with them.

Once I made it to the back ladder, I called up to Qidira. She lowered the basket that hung over the edge and I emptied the grapes into it, resting the bowl upside down on top of the harvest. She pulled all of it back up to the porch.

"Will you please get me something to wipe my feet with when I get up there?" I asked.

"Of course." She disappeared back inside. I was already at the top of the ladder by the time she returned with a rough cloth.

As I dried my feet, I said, "Qid, I have to go into the hills."

I did not know where to start my search, nor was I even sure I wanted to. But I remembered my father's words: *"Your job is to be of service. You owe your life to this universe. Never take that lightly."* I sighed.

"I want to come with you," Qidira said. Her words were not a plea for permission. They were a statement of action.

I stood up and looked sidewise at my dark-haired friend. Her face was a swirling mix of fear, sadness, and characteristic belligerence. I cocked my head to one side.

"I don't know, Qid—"

She cut me off. "I can do it. What, you think I can't?"

She put her hands on her hips in an all too familiar gesture of defiance.

"No, no, no," I said, trying to soothe her. "That's not it. Actually, I think you would be a big help. If there are dwarfs there, I will need you. And you know more about what it's like further into the mountains than anyone else down here. I just don't know if, if . . ."

I struggled for words. I was a solitary being, or so I thought. Qidira gave me a sense of home that was beyond measure, but when I went out to do a job or to take care of something, I did it by myself. This job—this *something*—was big. And I knew I would need all of my strength to carry it out. A niggling fear rose in my gut, escorted, however, by my baseline determination. I did not know what I was in for, and while that was okay for me, I did not want to risk Qidira's well-being.

"Qid, I cannot lose you. I just cannot, and that's that."

"And I'm supposed to be okay with losing you?" Her voice rose in pitch. "Every time you go into the forest, every time you go to do something for someone, I am scared I will lose you." She was yelling by now, gesticulating toward the trees and the town. "I pray, and I wait, and I cook . . . and you have always come back. But Elon, this time . . ." She stopped. She dropped her arms to her side and looked toward the mountains. "This time is different. This time it is not just about you. It is about me, too." She pointed a finger up and into my face. "I am going with you, and do not even argue again because I will win, oh yes, and you know it, too."

I tried not to smile. I raised my eyebrows and rolled my lips in between my teeth. "Uh . . . I guess that's final then."

She gave a solitary nod and moved past me into the house.

STROM

I washed the grapes and let Qidira put salve on my face. It did not need it by now, as my body was already reabsorbing the bruise, but I let her do it for the sake of peace.

"What is your plan for the rest of the day?" She focused on my face as she spoke.

"Strom's coming over."

Qidira smiled and nodded. I well knew her opinion of my one and only friend from town and I was grateful for her support. She said, "I will make something human-friendly for lunch."

"When do we not eat food that is human friendly?" I laughed, which must have caused my head to bounce because Qidira made a show of stopping the movement.

"Hold still. I'm almost done." She grasped my chin with her free hand.

"Sorry."

"What are you two going to do today?"

Luckily, I remembered Qidira's admonition to not move in time to keep myself from shrugging. "I don't know.

Last time we worked on take-down's. Maybe I'll finish his attack training."

Strom was the younger brother of the town's strongest fighter and hunter, Stahl. I was not a fan of Stahl, a fact I did my best to hide around the townsfolk. It was no secret that Stahl felt we were in competition any time we met. He was tall, but I was taller. He was blond, but my hair was lighter. He was strong, but my muscles were tougher. Perhaps most upsetting for the hunter, however, was that his brother had come to me to learn to fight.

Qidira put the lid back on her jar of salve. The minty, medicinal odor lingered and I knew it would permeate every inch of air I breathed for the rest of the day. "Just do not re-open any of those wounds," she said. "I think I got them on the road to healing."

I bit back my response. A natural caretaker, Qidira needed her victories. "I promise. Seriously, though, do you think he could land a blow hard enough to split my lip?" I chuckled at the thought of the short, scrawny Strom jumping high enough in the air to execute a round-house kick to my face.

Qidira gazed at me from under raised eyebrows. "With you as his teacher, my sweet friend. it will not take him long to learn."

Her confidence soothed my heart as if she applied balm there, too. "Thanks."

The sound of footsteps on the front stairs pulled us both from our moment. Together, we greeted the blond youth on the front porch.

"Hey, little man," I said as we hugged.

He snorted and looked me up and down. "Hey, Stretch."

I held my arms wide. "Look, I can't help it if the rest of you lack my genetic superiority."

Qidira slapped the back of her hand against my fore-arm. "Please. Everyone's little compared to you."

"Whatever makes you feel better, Qid."

This comment earned me a pursed-lip glare. "Come on inside," she cooed to our visitor.

"I say 'little' in the most loving way possible," I called after the duo. Qidira shut the door in my face before I could tell if the words made it to Strom's ears or not.

AFTER A HEARTY DOSE OF BEBI, Strom and I headed to the edge of the forest.

"Where are we going?" he asked as we waded through the soggy grass.

"To the forest." I did not turn around when I spoke, so, until I heard his voice from farther back, I did not know he had stopped walking.

"The forest?"

I looked over my shoulder to where he stood on a dry mound of sod. "Yeah. I figured we've done enough defensive work, I think it's time we perfect your offensive moves."

His face brightened but fear remained etched in his light features. "We've never gone into the forest before."

Internally, I rolled my eyes, but outwardly I floated back to where he waited. "It'll be all right, I promise. We're just going into the edge, not anywhere near Grod Mesto." He drew a quick intake of breath at the mention of the vamphyre settlement. I joined him in a sigh. My hurt at his continued fear of vamphyres lay hidden behind understanding. Still, it was there. "Vamps aren't all bad." I felt like I had uttered those words too many times in the last few weeks. I kept my voice low and nonthreatening, and I repeated it, yet again. "They're really not."

"I know," Strom said. He extended a hip out to one side and rested a hand on his hipbone.

I couldn't help myself. I said, "Oh man, you've been spending way too much time with Qidira."

He chuckled. "Shut up."

I jerked my head toward the thick line of trees in the distance. "Come on, don't worry." I floated a few feet off the ground. "What could go wrong?"

Again, he reminded me of Qidira as he glared at me from under furrowed brows. Still, he did not move. His features softened as he spoke again. "It's just . . ." His voice trailed away and he gazed at the forest. "The girl who was killed last week, the one left against the cliff base . . . she, I mean, I . . ."

He never finished his sentence. I gave him the space to speak, staying quiet for what felt like an eternity, but still he never told me what the girl was to him. I reminded myself not to make assumptions and decided to let the matter hang between us.

I gazed at the mountains, toward where the mangled body of the teenaged girl had been discovered. The image of her bloody body was sharp in my mind's eye. Her clothes had been soaked, standing out in crimson contrast to the pale, gray rocks of the mountainside.

"I'm sorry," I finally said.

Strom looked into my eyes. "I watched you retrieve her, but I just couldn't help."

I nodded.

"It's hard, you know?" he continued. "I know you, and you're not at all like them." He flicked his hand towards the forest. It was an angry, dismissive motion and I was reminded of his older brother.

I sighed, again. "I don't like all humans, but you seem okay." I smiled as I mirrored his contemptuous movement, only toward the village. He did not seem amused. "Look, I don't like your brother, you know that—"

"Stahl doesn't kill innocent people," Strom interrupted.

Stinging anger mingled with my hurt feelings. When I spoke, I didn't bother to keep the emotional edge from my voice. "Are you sure about that? What about that vamp he killed last year, huh? She had a child and a husband; did you know that? She never fed on any humans. Your brother hunted her down and killed her in cold blood. She was innocent." My chest heaved. I focused on calming my breathing and then repeated, my tone relaying my vulnerability, "Did you know that?"

Strom nodded, unphased. "I do, because you told me." He paused and we shared a few charged breaths before he continued. "How do we know that she wasn't the one who killed that family on the outskirts of town? She looked just like the vamp who did it."

I glared at him. The poor kid was simply sharing his feelings, ignorant and biased as they may have been. I could not blame him, just as I could not blame any of the other humans in the settlement. My heart suddenly ached for all of the hate and I felt defeated.

"All you humans look alike, too, so we best be sure I get the right one if there's ever a crime and I'm called to deliver the consequences. Now come on, you've got a big lesson in front of you today."

VISITORS

*R*uddy cheeked and worn out, Strom joined me as I returned home. I smelled the savory salmon before we reached the top of the stairs and my stomach growled as I pushed open the door.

"That smells amazing, Qid."

"It does," Strom echoed.

One step over the threshold and we both froze. Qidira's look stopped us like barbed wire and we backtracked, leaving our dirty boots next to a rocking chair outside.

Once sock-footed and in the delicious smelling warmth of the kitchen, I asked Strom, "Do you need to go home and change?"

He shook his head. "I'm good, thanks."

"We can hold dinner for you," Qidira offered.

I brushed drying mud off of his vest and it fell to the floor in orangish clumps. "Yeah, you don't want to let your dad catch you all mussed up."

"Hey," Qidira chastised. "I just cleaned the floors. What is wrong with you?"

"I'm an uncivilized animal, it's true." As if to punctuate my assertions, I snatched a knot of bread from a basket on the table and shoved the whole thing in my mouth. "You are amazing, Qid. These are phenomenal."

Qidira pinched her lips together and narrowed her eyes. Soon, she noticed Strom ogling the bread as well and released her ire. "Go ahead," she said to the youth. "You can have some, too."

Strom wasted no time in joining me in enjoying a fluffy roll. "Oh, my Gods, so good," he managed through a mouthful of bread.

Qidira rolled her eyes. "Strom, Elon is un-teaching you all of the manners your mother has worked so hard to instill. Be careful with that."

Strom smiled. Bits of bread dotted his white teeth. I simply opened my mouth and showed Qidira my own masticated snack.

"Gross," Qidira replied with a frown.

As we settled into the dinner proper, Qidira inquired about our day.

"He did well, actually," I responded, looking to Strom.

"Don't sound so surprised." He chuckled, and then finished his last bite of flaky fish.

I elbowed him playfully. "You did a great job using your size to your advantage. Qid, you should have seen him." I expounded on his prowess amongst the trees and complimented his quick reflexes when he struck back after an attack. "Don't tell your brother I said this, but I think you'll be a better hand-to-hand combatant than he is."

"Yeah, I won't tell him that. Can you imagine?" Strom said.

I thought back to our conversation about killing vamphyres and knew that, if given the chance, Stahl might actually come for me next.

❧

AFTER DINNER, we settled on top of the stairs and enjoyed the gathering dusk. Qidira brought mugs of grape juice and we sat in sated silence as the sky darkened.

I sighed and smiled, my recent dark thoughts forgotten. Happiness settled in my heart.

As if in reaction to the audacity of my enjoying a moment of contentment, a deafening noise cut through the peaceful chirping of the frogs. It was a deep sound, like wind blowing through a raging fire, only exponentially louder. Out in the marsh, the grass waved wildly and the water buckled like it was trying to escape back into the earth.

We all looked up and saw the source of the noise—a large ship was descending toward the bog. It was black and silver, with sharp angles, like a child had arrange triangle-shaped metal blocks into a piece of abstract art. Its descent slowed and soon it dropped into the soft ground.

We saw the wall of air moving toward us before we felt it. A wave of wind and water smacked into us and the house, and both Qidira and Strom were knocked backward. My fishing poles fell over, the wind chime swung wildly on its clear anchor. With a sharp crack, the front door banged against the inside wall. Luckily none of the windows shattered; I could only imagine how Qidira would have reacted to that. As it was, she grabbed my arm as I put a hand on the top railing post.

The noise stopped as suddenly as it started, and all I heard was the wind chime swinging around in its eerie attempt to find balance. In the distance, doors opened throughout the village and people yelled to one another. Out in the marsh, however, it was quiet. Even when three of the triangles dropped away from the ship and into the ground, no noise met our waiting ears.

Without speaking, I bolted to my feet and ran inside. I found my favorite knife under my mattress and sheathed it at my hip. As I descended the front stairs from the porch to the marsh, both Qidira and Strom followed.

With one foot still on the carved wood and one in the water, I turned and held up my hand, directing them to stop. "Stay here."

Qidira raised her eyebrows. A defiant half-smile curled one side of her mouth. "Um, no way. Are you crazy?"

"Less so when you're not around, and that's why I need you to stay here."

She put a hand on her hip, cocked it out, and glared at me. I was reminded of my earlier conversation with Strom. Qidira took in a breath as if she was going to say something but then closed her mouth.

"I'm coming with you," Strom asserted. He scampered down the stairs until he rested on the bottom level.

I shook my head. "No, you're not."

"But you said—" he began.

"I said you would be a great fighter, but you still need practice." I glanced over my shoulder. "Besides, we have no idea what's in that thing." I grasped his upper arms. His hands clenched into fists at his side and, despite the impending unknown, his fiery drive touched my heart. "I need you to go into town and get the elders." I pulled away but then thought of something else. "And you should probably get your brother." In response to his look of consternation, I added, "I'm just saying."

He scowled but did not argue.

Qidira moved to stand next to Strom. She wove her arms around his waist and he draped his arm over her shoulders. "Go," she said. "I will be here." She looked up at the young man's face. "Elon is right." In response to his petulant expression, her eyebrow shot up. "Don't look at me that way. I'm sure someone will come looking for you soon, anyway."

Once again, I gazed toward the center of town. From this distance I could just make out people rushing into the meeting hall. I turned back to Qidira. "Tell whoever shows up that I'll be back with more information."

I turned and started across the marsh.

I had not gone far when I sensed something radiating from the mass of metal. It wasn't a feeling I had experienced before and, as a result, I heightened my level of caution. I stooped and moved as best as I could through the marsh.

Like they're not going to see you coming. I laughed out loud at myself and returned to simply hovering over the ground.

When I reached the ship, I travelled around the awkward vessel, studying every angle. There were no windows and no doors that I could see. I took almost a hundred breaths to walk around the entire thing and still I found no port of entry. When I returned to the spot where I started, I stared at the dark metal. My father was able to tell things about objects, like who had owned them and where they had been, just by touching them. I had never been able to do it, and not for lack of trying. I thought this might be another opportunity to practice, so I pressed my hands against the ship and closed my eyes. I recalled what it felt like when I was communicating with the Sidar elder . . . I reached out with my mind, willing my DNA to bring forth a power I had never used.

Nothing happened. I placed my hands on my hips and shook my head.

Now what? What do I do now? Do I wait here? Do I go home and wait?

A noise of frustration escaped my lips. Waiting was not my strongest talent. I could wait if I were hunting something, if I was the unknown, but waiting, so exposed, was difficult.

In an effort to quiet my discomfort, my mind attempted to reason with me. *Something has to happen with this thing sooner or later.* If what I had to do was stalk it until it made the first move, well, that I could live with. I decided to return home, retrieve supplies, and wait on the edge of the woods.

Apparently, however, the ship had other plans. It was when I turned to walk back home that I felt the first contact. It was like a string was attached to the front of my chest and someone began pulling it through my body, out of my back, and into the alien structure. The power made me catch my breath and I stumbled.

Whoa.

I turned around and the lure lessened. I moved toward the vessel and the sense of pressure dissipated to almost nothing. Walking right up to the dark, silvery-black metal, I pressed my entire body against it, arms up in a position of surrender. I turned my face toward the ocean, laid my cheek against the cool craft, and closed my eyes.

Something surged through me, something that made me want to pull back. I remembered my encounter with the Sidar elder and stayed in contact with the ship. Focusing my thoughts, I reached out from everywhere in my body, through the metal, and into the ship. I thought my body was going to ooze through the hull, but it did not. Suddenly, the mental link ended.

Okay, concentrate. Think of the feeling you felt through the sect leader's hands.

I focused on that feeling of connection and something new happened: that sense of home I had when I slept crept over me.

Once I was standing in that feeling, my mind, or power, or whatever was going on, moved fully into the ship. I could see nothing, but I felt everything. The space was cold . . . no, lifeless. Then, like a flash of hot air, a blast of dark energy and a blur of thoughts resounded in my head. It left as soon as it arrived, and I was back to feeling the emptiness. I kept reaching, having to refocus when I distracted myself by reflecting on just how cool this new power was.

After a few breaths, I felt a rush of emotions. It was confusing, a muddled stew of multiple beings. Aside from it being hard to cope with so many voices in my head, I did not like what I was getting. I felt excitement and triumph, but there was also fear, hunger, lust, greed, and hate. I shuddered. At that moment, a stronger energy entered the space and uncertainty ensued. Everyone stopped, or at least I thought they did—each "presence" became stationary. Out of curiosity, I ventured further into the crowd.

Then I felt *it*—a harsh, malevolent presence reached out and touched my energy. Without a doubt, this new presence was one hundred percent vamphyre. At first, this new female essence stroked my psyche gently. It was a cold, investigatory caress. Soon, however, the feeling shifted from silky to abrasive as something rushed toward me. A high-pitched screech sounded in my head and something slammed into my chest. I flew backward, landing against a mound of earth, my lower torso in a murky puddle.

"What the Gods?" I exclaimed.

I sat there trying to catch my breath, trying to make sense of what just happened. My eyes focused once again on the towering hunk of hard angles in front of me.

I stumbled to my feet, as though someone might fly through the metal at any second. As I stood with my knife drawn, I realized I was breathing heavily. I focused on steadying my breath and wondered, *Why is no one coming out? They know I'm here now . . . why don't they show themselves?*

Soon, the invisible string pulled me forward once more and I reluctantly followed its not-so-subtle persuasion. I sheathed my knife and put my hands out in front of me; I did not want my whole body against that thing again.

When my hands touched the metal, I heard a new voice in my head. Warning and panic tinged the psychic communication. *"Join us now or walk away, Other. I know who you are and I do not want to harm you. You are part of us."* I felt a distinct twinge of heartache. *"But please beware—others here crave more from you. I do not want them to harm you; please do not get in the way. When we finish here, you can come with us. Go into the forest, stay there until I call to you."* Warning returned to the voice. *"Please be careful, though. Stay hidden."* At that moment, the malevolent presence reappeared and whatever connection I had vanished.

I was left standing in the setting sun, alone. Having multiple energies running through my mind had crowded my thoughts and now that they were gone, I felt strangely alone.

I looked around for some other sign of who was inside. I should have watched where I was going because, as I turned to head home, I fell over a rise and landed hard on my hands and knees in a pool of water.

Nice, I thought. *Smooth and intimidating.*

I got up and slid away from the ship. When I felt I was at a safe distance, I broke into a half-run, using what energy I had left to fly. I needed to get home. Whatever was in that thing, I was not hiding from it. I sure as hell was not going into the forest and waiting there for it. It felt like too much of a coincidence that the Sidar came to me just as this thing was about to land.

I had to go into the mountains.

MORE VISITORS

*A*s I approached the house, my desire to be ensconced in its warm safety called to me like never before. The lights inside burned brightly against the budding dusk. Flickering flames jumped from torches mounted on the porch railing. Qidira was pacing in the front room and I could make out other figures sitting at our table. Still a good five clicks away, I slowed my pace as Strom raced down the steps toward me.

"What is it?" he asked.

My mind concocted a myriad of possible responses. I decided that the truth, as I knew it, was probably the best. "I don't know."

Strom shot me a look that said, *"Don't lie."*

In spite of myself, I sneered. "I mean, I know there are people in there. Some Sidar-Other and, yes, some vamps." I left out the part about the sinister being. Given our recent discussion, I felt Strom needed nothing further to fear at that moment.

He seemed satisfied with my answer. "Okay. Come on, everyone's waiting."

He trotted back toward the house, hopping over wet ground and occasionally landing with a childlike splash. I smiled.

I knew who was at my kitchen table: at least one of the elders of the village, if not two, the shaman, and Stahl. In his burly, blondness, Stahl liked to claim to be pure human. My time with Strom, however, had given me doubts about the brothers. I did not feel Sidar in them, but Strom's spirit was that of an Other.

Until now, at least, I had done a good job at letting Stahl take care of threats to the village first. I jumped in only if necessary, cleaning up what he left, or what he decided he did not want to do. Really, he did what would get him attention and glory, and I did whatever he was too scared to tackle.

Qidira ran out of the door as I climbed the stairs. She stopped short of jumping on me. "Tell me what it is . . . quick, before we go in."

"Qid, I don't know what it is, really I don't. Let's just go inside and I'll tell them what they need to hear, and we can talk later."

She narrowed her eyes and pursed her lips before agreeing. "Okay."

Once inside, the three men at the table rose from their seats. Stahl was already standing and Strom took up his post behind his brother. I was right about who had been sitting in my dining room- it was, indeed, the elders and the shaman.

"Elon, tell us what you found." The oldest of the elders, Hanon, rushed forward as if to embrace me. When he reached me, however, he simply grabbed his own light brown hands and picked at his fingers. The other two who had been seated moved toward me, too, and I motioned for them to stop and sit down again. Stahl remained sentry-like in the background as I joined the humans at the table.

I did not know where to start, and while I wanted to tell them the truth, I did not feel like exposing my new power to them. The less they thought of me as Other, the more they would trust me.

"It's definitely a ship." My peripheral vision caught Qidira's eye-roll. She fixed me with a *thank you mistress obvious,* glare. I ignored her and continued. "It had no distinguishing markings, and I couldn't find any doors—at all. No one came out while I was there, and there was no noise. Honestly, I don't know who is in there."

I looked at Qidira for a long moment. She gave the slightest shake of her head that meant she did not want me telling them anything more. I widened my eyes as if to say, *I have to say something.* Then I raised an eyebrow and tipped my head to one side to communicate that she did not know what I knew, and she needed to wait her turn.

What was supposed to have been just a look between the two of us drew the attention of the whole room and everyone gazed from one of us to the other. Qidira dropped her eyes to the floor and I returned my attention to our visitors, taking in a deep breath.

"As you all know, I am part Sidar." There was a murmur of accord. "While I was out there I . . . sensed something. I can't tell you what it is, but I'm going to make my recommendations based on what I felt: take whoever will follow and go to the caves. Go to the mountains if you must, but I recommend that you go away until I can sort this out." A look of apprehension grew on the faces of the elders, and the shaman nodded like I had said something wise.

Stahl was the only one who seemed to disagree. He crossed his arms and widened his stance. It was my turn to roll my eyes. Behind his brother, Strom shook his head. I didn't have to read his mind to know he was warning me that this was not the time for a battle of wills.

"I'm not running from whatever this is," Stahl said.

"Surprise," Qidira muttered as if she meant for only me to hear and accidentally said it too loud. She looked up and flashed her sweetest smile.

"Whatever," I said. "I don't care what you do, but you"— I pointed at Strom— "need to go to the caves as well." I ignored his silent yet irritated response and focused my attention back on the three older men in front of me. "I have to go into the mountains." Hanon reached for my hand. His touch was warm, and unexpected. I looked around for Qidira and she walked up beside me.

"You cannot go," Hanon said. "You cannot leave us now, not with this." He gesticulated toward the ship. "You have always protected us, always done for the good of the settlement. You cannot just leave us unprotected."

At this, Stahl forcefully blew air out through his nose, and I saw where his arms were changing color from pressure where they were crossed.

I laughed to myself in an effort to restrain my belligerence. *No time to be childish*.

"My trip into the mountains is to benefit the whole settlement." At least I thought it might be. "And if you do what I suggest, you won't need me. Besides, there are plenty of men in the village to protect you all." I looked up at Stahl as I said this last part and then looked past him to his brother. I winked. The communication was not lost on Stahl, who turned around, his mouth gaping with incredulity.

"Don't tell me you've been . . ." Stahl started. He then spoke through gritted teeth. "I told you to stop training with her."

"Shut it," Qidira said. "This is no time for pride. Strom is a strong fighter and you will do well to allow him to help protect the village in this time of need. Send him with the people into the caves and he can help protect them there if anything should follow."

I thought a take-that glare might be too much for the muscly human, so I looked away. I leaned into Hanon and took his hands in mine.

"Listen: I don't know what is in there. From what I can tell, I don't like it. I think there is something in the mountains that can help us, and I must find it. If nothing else I *will* find more Sidar and perhaps they will agree to help should we need it." Not that I could imagine the wispy empaths leaving the safety of their caves, but it sounded good at the time.

At the suggestion of full-blooded Sidar coming down out of the hills, the two elders exchanged anxious glances. Full-blooded Sidar are peaceful and community-oriented, but the humans' fear continued to reign. Again, the shaman nodded as if my wisdom never stopped flowing.

Stahl strode forward and began, "Elder Hanon, I believe——" but Hanon cut him off with a hand gesture and we never learned what Stahl believed.

Hanon folded his hands in front of his belly. "*I* believe that this young woman has never done us wrong." He directed the next part to me. "We will go. We will take who we can and we will join those that have already moved into the caves. Go into the mountains; take what you need from the village. Just come and find us when you are done." With that, he stood. The other men stood, too, and followed him as he made for the door.

Before the left, Hannon stopped, and said, "Elon, I hope you find what you are looking for."

The only movement was the bobbing of the shaman's

head. It made me want to strangle him. Instead, I said, "Thank you." They turned and passed through the front door, to the porch.

Stahl was the last to leave. He paused at the threshold and said, "Don't let us down. I can fight whoever comes our way, but——" his voice faltered and dropped into an awkward cadence, "I'm not you."

"Uh . . .," was all I could manage in response.

Strom flashed me a victorious grin.

Qidira jumped in. "Stahl, you do your part and we will do ours. Trust us and we will, well, we will come find you when we are done."

Stahl pulled himself back up to his full height and looked from Qidira to me, and back again. "Until then, may the Gods keep you well." With this, he turned and hurried after the rest of his party.

"I'll check in tomorrow," Strom managed before his brother yanked him outside by his arm.

Qidira rushed forward and shut the door. I moved around the room extinguishing all of the flames until the only light in the room was that of the outside torches.

"Wow," I said, blowing out the last candle. "A Gods bless you and everything. I'm impressed—never thought he had it in him."

Qidira pulled me toward a couch near the front door. It sat at an angle, spanning the southwest corner. Behind it lived a flowering jasmine bush that always seemed in bloom.

The soft material gave way as I sank into the over-stuffed seat. Soon, however, the scent of the jasmine over-whelmed me and my mind clouded. "Qid, can we not sit here?"

She looked around and realized what she had done. "Oh," she said, "of course."

We moved back to the table and I sat down as Qidira fetched us fresh tea. Now that it was dark, I needed to be able to see the ship. The torches outside were high enough that the glare did not impede my view. I kept my eye on the massive structure as I told Qidira about what happened in the marsh. I even told her the part about tripping, the retelling of which she found only mildly amusing. She definitely did not think it was as funny as I did looking back.

"Okay, let me get this right—you projected your psychic *feelers* into this ship? You interacted with whoever is in there?"

"Uh, yup." I kept my gaze trained on the hulking, alien vessel. "There are Sidar in there. They weren't pure Sidar, but they knew me, and worried for me, as only other Sidar can." I looked toward her now and found her staring intently at my face. "Qid, I felt vamps, too. They tried to control me, but I think the Sidar interceded . . . I don't know. One of them told me to leave, and I can only imagine that was because whoever is in charge has plans for this settlement, or maybe the humans who live in it. It was weird though, like the one I interacted with wasn't supposed to be talking to me."

Qidira sat like a statue. She stared into my eyes. "That is a vamp-made ship. You know it and so do I. I saw your face when it landed; I know you've seen one like it before."

She was right, I had. Similar vessels fell from the sky on the planet where I lived with my parents. They descended from the stars, landing on the mainland. For a few nights after they arrived, we heard screaming, and then it would be silent. The ships stayed for seven sunsets and then left with a roar of fire. The land burned for three days until a storm came and the rain extinguished the blaze. The first time it happened, I was young and afterward, my parents intensified my education. Not just about science, but about my heritage and natural defenses. It was then that my father taught me one of his most valuable lessons.

"Choose wisely, Hoshi. Do not underestimate yourself, or your enemy. Power is unpredictable and those who wield it can be cunning. With every choice you make, you alter the outcome. Choose wisely."

These memories flooded back as I ruminated on my new power. *Unpredictable.* That word rang through my head like a warning and for the first time in my life, I feared myself.

Was I strong enough? I mean, who thought it was a good idea to give me more power? I shook my head and pushed the image of my father's pale face from my mind.

"I know that look," Qidira said.

"What?" I replied, my defenses triggered.

"You're thinking about your parents."

For at least the third time that night, I rolled my eyes, but I did not argue with her. The last memory I had of my father stabbed my heart—his eyes closed, laying in the fire's glow as his breathing stopped. I could not handle that pain at the moment.

I swallowed hard and returned to our discussion. "I know this psychic feeler thing is an extension of my Sidar connection, but with that I should have only been able to sense the other Sidar. Maybe the ship contains something like a cognitive and emotional energy soup made up of the Sidar powers and the vamp abilities?"

More unbidden memories of my parents hijacked my consciousness. One theory they routinely expounded upon was that being mixed was not just about what the individual parts of my heritage could bring, but how those parts interacted to create something new, something better. They taught me that I was not just a watered-down version of the original. I was something new.

"Elon, I don't know. The other Sidar mixes I have met

do not seem to have that power, even the ones with the vamphyric virus."

"Vamps can control minds, which means they have to be able to read them, at least a little. The Sidar can send out messages from who knows how far away, and, as I learned last night, they can pool their power and physically project someone." My mind raced with what I knew about vamphyric inheritance patterns, about the virus and its effects on humans versus Other.

I knew that because I had the vamphyre virus already in my genetic code when I was born, I had a certain degree of immunity. I thought about what my mother taught me about virology and I had to wonder, was the virus I held mutating? Would it continue to do so? What else might change? And what happened if I managed to contract another strain, how would they interact?

Qidira interrupted my mental churning. "All fine and good, great, whatever. You know as well as I do that the vamps that are in that thing"—she jabbed a finger in the direction of the ship— "are not here on a goodwill mission. We need to go. You said it yourself—we must find the Sidar and figure this all out. It's too much of a coincidence that the Sidar contacted you for help just as the vamps landed."

"I know, I had the same thought. That's why I said: we have to go into the mountains, as soon as we can. Get some stuff together; gather food and clothes, but we might need your metallurgical skills, so bring whatever it is you need."

She looked at me from under lowered eyebrows as if to say, *you know I cannot bring what I need.*

"Or we will find it in the hills, whatever," I added in my ignorance. "Please just get me whatever weapons you've been working on."

She smirked, jumped from her chair, and rushed up to

her room. I watched her go and then turned my attention back to the marsh. I hoped that what I sensed was the extent of who was in that ship. In my gut, however, I knew it wasn't.

My father's words rang in my mind for the second time in as many hours: *Don't underestimate yourself, or your enemy.*

I knew with certainty that soon I would have to confront whoever hid inside the dark metal craft.

I sighed. *Well, here we go.*

THE FIRST STRIKE

Our gear was piled by the back door, ready for our descent down the ladder to the boardwalks that wound around and through the town, but we knew we needed rest before we set out.

"Sleep," Qidira soothed me from where she sat on the side of my bed. "It will help prepare you for whatever comes our way."

Her fingers danced over my back, tracing dwarfen runes against my thin undershirt. The feeling calmed my tumultuous thoughts and I gave in to drooping eyelids.

My eyes were closed for only mere seconds, however, before shrieks from the center of town penetrated my calm. When I jumped from bed, Qidira was already at the window. Her eyes bored through the blackness outside, trained on dancing flames that licked the darkness of the moonless night.

"They are in the sky." Qidira's voice held an unfamiliar fear. Still, she stood like a sentinel, staring at the bobbing torches that rushed through the village. As if held by spectral hands, the chaotic line of light led to the large fire at the edge of town.

More screams reached us. Shadows swooped from hidden roosts, their sinister darkness visible even with no moon. Then a heart-wrenching sound filled my ears. It was the cry of loss. The all too familiar verbalization of unrestrained grief.

I pulled on my toughest leather garb and gathered my hair in a messy ponytail at the back of my head. "Stay here."

I wasn't sure Qidira would listen, as she rarely did, but this time she simply nodded. As I sped from the room, she touched my arm. "Be careful."

With heretofore unknown speed, I shot like an arrow out of the house and toward the center of town. As I honed my senses in on the sound that rang through the chaos like no other, I focused on reaching my goal. Thus distracted, I did not sense the approaching energy before it was nearly too late. Halfway to town, a figure dove at me through the darkness and I reacted without thought.

Dropping to one knee, I pulled a dagger from my leg sheath and aimed for the heart. Bone cracked as my knife found its mark. The momentum of both our actions drove my hand past the penetrated breast bone and into the attacker's chest cavity. Warm liquid pulsed against my face in spurts. I felt it run downward, past my elbow. The blood reached my underarm and saturated my undershirt. The vamphyre had no time to scream before he fell dead against me.

I shoved him off and he tumbled to the slatted wood. I took but a moment to consider the crumpled body on the boardwalk. His sharp features were pale, with a familiar facial ridge visible running from his forehead to his cheek. His hair belied his vamphyre heritage, however, as thick, dark strands lay strewn over his shoulders and covered one of his eyes.

I sighed. A pang of sadness filled my gut for the loss of a Sidar Other, but I remembered my own words: *while not all vamphyres are bad, some of them are.*

With one last glance at my attacker, I continued toward town. As I approached, Stahl's deep voice rang through the cacophony. "Find Hanon, take him to the caves. Everyone, go, now." He ushered townsfolk along as they made their way to the base of the cliffs, where the mountains met the sea. "Strom, now, let's go. Strom!"

I scanned the crowd for the familiar mop of blond. Soon, I saw my friend darting in and around three darkly-clad aggressors. Stahl saw him, too, and made it to the struggle before I did. In one fluid movement, he landed a deadly blow with an axe through the neck of one enemy.

As I joined the fight, Stahl moved toward the next vamphyre, so I headed for the third. Seeing she was outnumbered, she took to the air before I reached her. My moment of relief at her withdrawal was annihilated when I saw Strom's feet leave the ground. I lunged to grab his legs but was too late.

"Strom!"

Both Stahl and I yelled his name at the same time as the dark figure flew away with the young man in her grasp. As if her departure was a call to retreat, the other attackers shot into the night, leaving their mangled prey bleeding in the darkness.

"NOTHING?" Stahl stopped pacing the central square the moment he saw me approach.

"I'm sorry. Nothing." The sun hovered low beyond the

horizon, threatening us with a new dawn and I still had not found Strom. "It wasn't the Palusian vamps." Not that I thought the attack had been orchestrated by the local vamphyre sect, but still, it was at least somewhere to start.

Stahl looked over my shoulder toward the marsh. His lip twitched at one side and he released a low growl. "You must go back to the ship."

Exasperation dripped from my words. "I can't, don't you understand? What is on that ship is too powerful for me. Even the Sidar know it." I gestured toward the mountains. "They called to me last night, wait, the night before, or was it two days ago? Whatever, I can't seem to keep my days straight anymore. They told me they needed my help and it can't be a coincidence that it happened right as the ship arrived."

Stahl considered my face. The muscles in his jaw flexed and relaxed as he clenched his teeth. Anger flashed in his eyes. "This is your fault."

While I should have seen this coming, it still caught me off guard. "Seriously? Which part, the ship or the attack last night?"

"Strom trusted you. He told me you thought he was a strong fighter." His agitation grew as he stepped closer. "You filled his soft mind with lies and he thought he could fight them. Whatever happens to him, it's on you." His hot breath blew against my face.

I reminded myself it was his grief talking. At least mostly his grief; his baseline hate for vamphyres and Other still remained, that much was clear. Keeping my voice low I said, "Perhaps if you had taught him to fight as he requested, this wouldn't have happened." My own grief had taken over and the words escaped my lips against my will.

I had a moment to reflect on my lack of control over

my mouth before Stahl's fist landed against my jaw. Caught off guard, I stumbled. His howl of pain, tinted with rage at his physical impotence in this situation, verified my next thought: his action hurt him more than me.

Bent around his broken hand, Stahl glared up at me. "You had better find him or I will kill you myself."

"He was my friend, you know." My own sense of powerlessness seethed in my chest. My resolve to go into the mountains, to find the Sidar and learn what they knew, tightened like a stone belt around my heart.

Again, Stahl's lips twitched at one side. "Vamphyres don't have friends. They only have prey."

INTO THE MOUNTAINS

"id you lay him out on the boardwalk?" Qidira stood waiting as I completed the check of my gear. Her hands rested on her hips and I could tell that, had she been there, those small fists would have found their way to Stahl's face.

"I didn't. He's grieving, Qid. I know that kind of fear and me punching him would not have done any good." I stood up and reconsidered. "Okay, perhaps it would have done me a small amount of good."

Qidira pursed her lips and nodded as she shouldered her own gear.

"Ready?" I asked.

"Yup. You?"

"As I'll ever be."

The marsh was quiet as we wound our way through the maze of bridges and walkways toward town. It was as if even the birds and plants mourned the village's loss. We stopped at the site of my first attack hours earlier.

"That's a lot of blood," Qidira observed.

All that was left of my kill was a maroon stain, which

was already being absorbed by the wood. "His comrades must have retrieved the body." Years of rain would never wash that color away and I reflected that when we came back, if we made it back, I would need to remove it.

Qidira tipped her head toward a spire of smoke past the village, at the mountain base, which curled toward the cloudy morning sky. "I think it is the townspeople. They're burning the vamps' bodies."

"I hope they protected themselves against contamination."

As we continued our movement along the boardwalk, I felt torn. I did not want to leave; I wanted to stay and be ready to fight the minute the aggressors appeared again. Despite their prejudice, I felt responsible for these people who had trusted me with their lives and opened their village to me when I arrived. At the same time, my gut told me that, no matter what my parentage, facing what was in that ship on my own—or worse, with other humans beside me—would not turn out well for me, or anyone with me.

Qidira and I had spent the last few hours of darkness double checking our supplies for the journey. We watched the ship for activity and it was at full daybreak that we had set out through the town. Some of the houses were shut up, still others stood open, abandoned in the heat of the attack.

As we approached the town hall, crying rose from a knot of people gathered on the expanse of wood that created a town square. It was the site of my last conversation with Stahl hours earlier. In the center, a scrub tree stood sentry to the town's activity. Scrawny and alone, it rose from the marsh and through the fashioned wooden walkway as if it alone dared challenge the town's design.

As we drew closer, I saw blood on the thin trunk of the tree. Sprawled against its base was a body, its legs strewn at unnatural angles. Crimson liquid soaked the fabric of the man's pants and I knew he was already dead. When we reached the crowd, they parted to allow me access. His face was unrecognizable, like the belly of a large, poorly cleaned fish. Bits of bone jutted from his macerated flesh where his nose used to be, his lips were missing and there were no eyes.

Animals always go for the soft parts first, I mused.

Soon, I noticed the hair. Matted as it was with blood, the hair was all too familiar. As the pieces came together, I launched myself the remaining few steps and scooped the young body into my arms. I felt Qidira's hand on my shoulder as my tears came.

I rocked there on the wood until a hand clamped on my upper arm and pulled me backwards. Annoyed at the interruption of my grief, I looked up into another familiar face. I felt a growl reach my throat but swallowed it at the site of Stahl's eyes, bloodshot and sleepless.

"Stahl, I . . ."

His face registered what I had clasped to my breast as he, too, recognized the dead youth's hair. Yet another howl of loss echoed through the empty town. His guttural cry raised in pitch until it climaxed as rage.

I pulled myself to my feet, ready for another attack. I cradled what was left of Strom but braced myself, willing to accept Stahl's barrage of fists. None came. Instead, tears fell down his beefy cheeks. Soon, his eyes rested once again on his brother and he reached a hand toward a patch of blond that was free of blood.

I kept my voice soft as I pulled the body out of his reach. "Don't."

Qidira laid a hand on his arm, and said through her own tears, "The virus."

The anger and confusion that clouded Stahl's eyes were

soon replaced with understanding. Looking from her, to me, and then to his brother, Stahl nodded. He stepped back and addressed the crowd. "Did anyone see what happened here?"

I shook my head. "This didn't happen here; there's not enough blood. No, they left him here after . . ." I swallowed hard.

One woman stepped forward. "Most people were gone by sunrise, but I kept my family inside until the sun came up, I wasn't taking any chances." I recognized her as the sister of the victim I avenged two nights prior. "This morning we came out in a group, on our way to follow the others, and we found him here."

Qidira bent down and picked up something that had been hidden under the body. It was a stone carving, with one large, round center and three orb-like projections attached at even intervals. "Elon?"

I studied the artifact without touching it. "I don't know. I've never seen it before. You?"

She peered at the object. "I know I have it on the roof of the house, but I cannot remember where it comes from . . . Wait, yes I do." She frowned at the item. Her brow pinched together.

"And?" I had no patience left, for anything, at that moment.

Her eyes met mine. "The Sidar. Amil used to have this same symbol on his alter…" Again, she gazed at the effigy in her hand.

In reaction to Stahl's look of rage, I said, "This wasn't the Sidar. No, they're not capable of this."

Stahl studied my eyes for a long few breaths before he spoke again. "At this point, I'm not sure of anything anymore."

The human woman who had spoken cried and turned

away. She buried her face into the chest of a young man near her who I guessed was her son.

Speaking to the crowd, I instructed, "All of you need to go to the caves, now. And yes, only come out in the daylight." I watched as they gathered their belongings and moved toward where the mountains met the sea.

Some gave backward glances at me and the body. Others simply looked back at the town. One girl turned and met my eyes. She was a pale, blonde-haired child who appeared to be an early teen. I felt something come from her, like a promise to be with us in spirit. She must have been a distantly mixed Sidar-Other who was passing for pure human because I had never heard of her or sensed her presence. This new discovery, that I was working to protect at least one family of Other as they lived in secret, strengthened my sense of purpose.

When they disappeared from sight, Qidira asked Stahl, "What would you like to do?"

His face remained twisted with emotion. "I don't know."

Surprised yet understanding of his indecision, I offered a solution. "Let's take him to the base of the mountains. He loved the waterfall there. We can bury him on the shore."

Stahl helped Qidira carry my portion of our traveling supplies and we finished our trek through the town, to the river. We moved to where the river emerged from a deep gorge and dug a grave in the soil near the rock face. We lowered the boy into the wet earth and Qidira placed the statue on his chest.

"Are there any prayers your people say?" I asked Stahl.

He sniffed, drawing in a full breath as if to steady himself. "May the sun always warm your face, may the wind be always at your back, and may the earth rise to meet you wherever you go."

"I'm not sure I would always want the sun in my face," Qidira mumbled at my elbow. I gave her a sharp jab.

"Would you like to say something?" Stahl offered. My surprise must have shown on my face because he added, "You were his friend. He loved you."

I was lost for words, embarrassed by my years of petty competition with this now grieving man, the only living reminder of my friend.

Qidira came to my rescue by uttering a prayer in an ancient dwarfen dialect. Peace settled over the space and we all stood, wordlessly listening to the falling water. I followed a twig with my eyes as it crested the top of the waterfall, fell into the frothy basin, and moved off to the east, where it meandered into the marsh. Looking up the river into the mountains, I peered into the deep gorge with its steep, rocky walls covered with moss and plants that managed to find a spot to hang on.

As the ground rose, a series of smaller waterfalls brought the water down to where we were. Directly in front of us, to the left of the burbling cascade, crude steps, created when erosion exposed underlaying stone and roots, led up and into the ravine. I gazed into the misty darkness. Two hundred clicks up, the gorge bent around toward the west and the water disappeared from sight.

Eventually, I broke the sacred silence. "I will find who did this. I promise."

Qidira linked her elbow through mine and leaned against my arm.

"I know you will," Stahl replied. He held out a hand for me to shake.

"Wait." I bent to the water and washed blood and dirt from my skin. Straightening up, I took the proffered gesture. I even let him squeeze me harder than I squeezed him. I thought it was only polite to let him win, at least once.

With one last bob of our hands, Stahl broke the connection. "We will wait for your return." He turned and followed his brethren towards the caves.

"Wow," I commented. I watched the hunter's blond head until he disappeared around a stone outcropping of the mountain.

"Come on," Qidira urged. "Let's get started."

As we entered the high-walled crack in the mountains, it did not take long to lose direct sunlight. The wet air was rich with the smell of soil, moss, and algae. The water next to us, clear and inviting, allowed us to see the bottom of the falling river. Scattered pebbles and sand littered the flat stone. At the base of each waterfall, a small pool collected the falling bubbles in a smooth, round-bottomed depression, where centuries of agitation had etched out a deep divot in the rock.

We did not speak as we climbed to the bend in the gorge. Once there, we paused and looked back toward the town, or what we could see in the small sliver of sunlight at the end of this cool, wet tunnel. Overhead, a bird cried in the trees. It reminded me that there were other living things here with us and I wondered if we might encounter another person.

Qidira must have read my mind because she said, "Do you want to change?"

I looked down at my shirt, still coated in Strom's blood. "Yeah, thanks."

After exchanging my undershirt for a clean one, I washed my leather over garments in the water. Unable to bear keeping the blood-stained soft material, I dropped my original shirt into the cold water and let it float over the next waterfall. Eventually it would land next to Strom's grave.

When I stood up, I felt cleansed and was ready to move on. As I shouldered my gear once again, a strange tingle tickled my skin.

Noticing my pause, Qidira asked, "What's the matter?"

"I feel something. It's thick on my skin but at the same time feels like it's barely touching me." That sounded crazier out loud than it had in my head.

But Qidira did not miss a beat. "Do you feel it stronger in either direction?"

I put down my pack again and moved onto an outcropping of rock. From there it was only a short jump to the other side.

"Anything?" she asked.

"Not really." I hopped to the other side of the water and climbed a pile of rock chips and stones that had fallen from the high walls and collected at the base. My footing was precarious, but soon I reached the gorge wall. Still, I could not feel a difference.

"Wait." I closed my eyes and touched the side of the ravine. I tried to push my mind into the rock, as I had the ship, but I did not get far. I turned around and half-walked, half-slid down the rock pile and back to Qidira.

I moved to the rock behind her and spread my hands wide. I closed my eyes and tried to convince myself that I could replicate what I had done in the marsh. It did not work.

"You said there were Sidar in the ship when you used your new power," Qidira said. "Maybe that enhanced your abilities? Like when they brought you to them. Maybe that took everyone in the room pooling their power to do it?"

"That's a good thought."

I rejoined Qidira on the path, put my hands on my

hips, and looked up to the sky. A slice of blue was visible through the overhanging trees that grew at the top of the gorge. I took a slow, deep breath in through my nose. The same tingle I had felt on my skin tickled my nose. A sneeze emerged in my throat as the sensation traveled to my chest. No sneeze came, though. The feeling dissipated as it spread through my body to my fingers. "It's something in the air. Not just on my skin . . . no, wait, this is different . . ." I told her about the sensation. "It's like an irritant, almost chemical. I don't know if that makes any sense."

"Sure, it does," she assured me. "But does it tell us we are going in the right direction?"

"Do we have a choice?"

"Actually, I was thinking that the people you saw were in a cave . . . maybe there is access to them through the cave system where the humans are now hiding?"

"Perhaps, but something told me to come into the mountains, and not *into* like through a door in the side, but into like up and into. We haven't even reached the lake at the first settlement yet. Let's get up there and stay for the night. Maybe the Sidar will come to me in my sleep again and give us a better sense of what to do."

The noise of debris cascading down the rock face where I stood moments earlier carried across the water. We both looked up. I thought I caught a hint of movement, but as a breeze shifted the trees, I convinced myself it had been the wind.

"Did you see that?" I asked.

"Yes." Qidira's eyes narrowed and her lips moved. "And I do not believe we should talk ourselves out of it. I don't know what your instincts are telling you, but mine say we are not alone."

Sure enough, I knew someone had been watching us.

WE GATHERED our supplies and continued up the trail. It took us a few thousand breaths to traverse a short distance; the footing was slippery and an old rockslide meant we had to climb boulders. Actually, I climbed and Qidira clung to my backpack.

The water found its way through the rocks just fine, but there still was a deeper than usual pool collecting on the other side. We stopped to rest and eat. We enjoyed smoked fish that Qidira brought and we drank from the river. The water was clear and crisp, yet round and smooth, like the feeling licorice leaves in my mouth after I eat it.

We packed ourselves back up and continued further into the mountains. After a while, the climb leveled out and, ahead of us, we saw a clearing in the trees. We first heard the rush of a large waterfall, and then, when we came around a small bend in the path, we saw the abandoned settlement.

The scene was breathtaking. Hills to the left and right of us sloped upwards, not gently so, but enough that one could climb out that way if needed; the sides of the valley were covered with a mixture of deciduous and evergreen trees. The most beautiful and impressive site, however, was a large waterfall. Not only was it wide but it was tall, and it did not just fall over the top of the mountain, it seemed to emerge from the rock itself. Towering above it was another craggy spire, which continued to angle away from us, stretching toward the sky. A cap of snow was just visible where the peak disappeared into the hazy blue of the upper atmosphere.

The cascading torrent fell into a deep, round lake, and on either side of the water lay evidence of the long-gone past inhabitants. The sun had risen to just past mid-day and bright yellow sunlight reflected off of the water. The lake narrowed as it approached us and we saw the sandy bottom as the river flowed over a short, thin waterfall directly in front of us, which could not have been more than three feet high because Qidira could see over it into the settlement.

"Look, Qid, it's your size." I pointed at the small waterfall.

"Yeah, and I bet you are under some illusion that that one"—she pointed toward the larger falls— "is your size?"

With a shrug, I said, "What can I say?"

Our laughter sang brightly around the valley.

THE FIRST SETTLEMENT

a crude but sturdy lumber bridge spanned the top of the smaller falls, connecting one side of the village to the other. The path we were on took a steep climb upwards and veered to the left, shortly splitting into a second trail to the right, over the bridge. We followed the main path up and got a full view of the valley. The water in the lake was dark, even with the sun shining directly on it. It was greener the deeper it got until I could see nothing at all.

What used to be a worn path leading away from the bridge was grassy but still discernible. It led toward what appeared to be the central gathering point. In the center of the shore on that side of the lake was a large pit, obviously once used as the settlement's main fire. Despite the surrounding overgrowth of flora, nothing seemed to have grown in the dark ashes. It stood like a foreboding scar amidst the otherwise green lakeside.

A few homes dotted the tree line, but they were small and few. Halfway to the base of the large waterfall, closer to the edge of the trees, an oblong trough carved out of one, immense granite boulder shone bright against the surrounding dilapidation. It stood on stone feet that curved out from the main structure. From this distance, it appeared to be a water trough.

I elbowed Qidira in the shoulder and pointed to the stone structure. "What's that?"

"I don't know."

She wandered closer to it, and I followed. As we passed the houses near the edge of the forest, it felt eerie to be back here. The saturated grass had grown high, and it obscured most of the doorways. Windows were broken in every frame, and some of the roofs had collapsed.

"It is something that I have not seen before," Qidira said, indicating to the stone basin. "It was not here when I was." When we drew closer, she lowered her bags to the ground. "Of course, it is dwarf made," she continued. "It would have taken a human too long to do this, and they could never have gotten it so *smooth*." She ran her hand along the edge as she walked the length of the trough. She turned to me when she reached the end and said, "It is ceremonial, but for what purpose, I do not know." She traced her hands back and forth over the flattened top, enraptured.

"Huh," I grunted, contemplating the stone. I saw etching around the bottom, and as I squinted to get a better look, Qidira leaned forward.

"There's no water. It rained two nights ago, there should be water here," she said.

"Did you see the symbols or writing or something along the base?" I squatted to get a better look.

The symbols looked vaguely familiar, close to runic writing, but some of the characters were just that little bit different that I could not read it. While I was familiar with most of the known alphabets, I had mostly learned the original, formal letters. It would have been impossible for me to account for any change or drift in the languages.

When Qidira did not answer, I looked up. "Qid . . ." I let out a short whistle when, again, she did not respond. "Hello, my friend . . ." I said in a sing-songy voice. "Come here."

As if shaken awake, she raised her head. Her eyes widened and she blinked repeatedly. Taking her hands from the stone, she joined me where I stood in the high grass. She lifted her skirts to kneel next to me and as she ran her fingers over the writing, she muttered something under her breath. Lines showed on her forehead as she furrowed her brow deeper and deeper in concentration. I, too, reached out and touched the stone. I instantly felt a shock, though, and drew my hand back.

"Woof," I said. "What the heck was that?" I looked from my fingers to the basin.

Qidira looked up at me. "What did you say?"

"That thing shocked me when I touched it. Why didn't it do that to you?" I stood up.

"I don't know." Distracted, she turned back to the rock. "I don't know . . ."

"Girl, get away from that thing." I grabbed her arm and yanked her back. "It's got some power over you and you're starting to freak me out."

Standing up as well, she rubbed her knees through her skirts and took in a deep breath. She looked around, taking in more of the scene then I think she had at first.

"I don't know, Elon."

"I know, you've said that already. What *do* you know? What are you feeling? What's going on? Why couldn't I touch it?"

"Umm . . ." She narrowed her eyes and turned toward the water. "I know that I want to get to the other side of that lake, away from here. As for why you could not touch it, I can only guess that it holds unique magic. Something in *it* did not like something in *you*."

I was oddly offended and I think my face betrayed my emotions because Qidira said, with a laugh in her voice, "It's only a freaking magic stone basin, get over it."

We grabbed our gear from the grass and headed back to the bridge.

As I followed Qidira, I said, with a defensive huff, "Well, what's wrong with me?" I imbued my voice with a playful hint of hurt, as I continued, "Magic has always liked me before."

She was moving quickly and even with her short step, I had to trot to catch up with her as she crossed the bridge.

"What's wrong with you, my sweet angel friend, is that you are part vamp, part Sidar, and part troll. There are plenty of reasons why a dwarf-made magic bowl might not want you to know its secrets. Or do you forget that Sidar can read objects? Or that vamps can control minds, even the minds of dwarfs if they are caught unawares?" We reached the other side and she stopped, turning around abruptly. I had to catch myself on the ends of the bridge railings. I ended up on the balls of my feet, hovering over her.

"But I'm not those things, I don't do those things." My voice sounded more defensive then I meant it to.

"And you expect a magic piece of stone to keep that in mind, do you? An object only has a brain of its own when someone uses it to channel themselves, and you know that. And then whoever it is channeling would have to be part Sidar themselves in order to feel what you were feeling, right? Well, apparently this thing isn't that smart, so get over it." She turned around again and moved toward the dwellings on that side of the lake.

The houses were arranged in increasingly larger arcs with the front row holding only four single-room dwellings. In the center of the arc, closer to the water, was a flat, long, stone table. There were no chairs, but I remember from when I had been here before that there had been rotting food on that table. Crows had been busy pulling at what was left behind. That had been a few years ago, and now, the table was clear.

Qidira set her bags down on the stone slab, and then she took off her leather shoes and tied up her skirts between her legs. Wading into the lake, she splashed water onto her still muddy knees.

I moved to explore the decaying dwellings. The first door I encountered was hanging from only one of three metal hinges. Inside, animal droppings littered the floor. An old bed sat in the opposite corner but one of the legs that used to support it had rotted and the bed lilted down toward me. Next to the stone hearth, there was an empty cradle. My heart ached and I moved on to the next home.

This one had no door. There was also nothing left inside, so I kept going. When I reached the third house, I saw that not only did this structure have a door, but the door was closed. This surprised me, and I peered inside through a broken window. All of a sudden, a startled rush of feathers flapped past my face, sending me jumping backward. I cursed. Looking up, I saw a gray morning bird flutter to the top of the next house. Qidira heard my expletive and asked what happened.

"Nothing, just a bird. It startled me is all. I guess I just didn't expect anything to be living here, not even animals."

I moved back to the door and took my time opening it, scared it might fall apart in my hands. It swung outwards with minimal effort and very little sound. Inside I found a neat room, set up like the first home I had seen—only this one was intact and there was no empty cradle. A double bed adorned the corner opposite the door. It had a mattress on it but no bedclothes. Directly to my left, a table was upright under the front window, and there were three chairs pushed in under it. Taking up most of the left wall, next to the bed was the stone fireplace. It was just like the one in the prior home, except this one contained ashes.

I knelt by the wide hearth, checking to see if the burned remnants might still be warm. They were not and I suddenly felt stupid for even thinking they might have been.

Qidira's shadow fell over the room as she stood in the doorway. "It looks like someone has been here, huh?" She moved into the room, too.

"But I don't think anyone *lives* here," I said. "Unless they take their sheets and blankets with them every time they leave for the day." I touched the table. A thin layer of dust coated the wood, disrupted only by a chaotic pattern of bird tracks.

I looked around and found a nest built on top of a cupboard in the back corner. "Someone hasn't been here in at least a season; the birds wouldn't have stayed otherwise."

"Well, let's not disturb the scary beasts anymore," Qidira said. "The next house has a door, too, but there is very little left inside, only a few scattered pieces of broken wood. I brought our stuff in there and have started to set up. It is still early so why don't you wash off in the lake and then look around to see what kind of sustenance you can find."

Outside, the sun rested above the trees on the other side of the valley. I shielded my eyes against the glare and moved toward the water. Stopping at the table, I took off all of my clothes except my undergarments. I thought I would feed two birds with one seed and wash both myself and my underwear, so I could have clean underclothes for the morning

As I waded into the water, I noted that the bottom of the lake was covered by sand. I brushed some away, trying to see what the silty substance sat on. I found smooth rock, like the rest of the river base. I carefully waded deeper, until the water hit my waist. I looked down and saw my feet. From the shore, the lake looked so dark I assumed that it must be silty, which would account for its dark color. The water so far was clear, however. *This sucker must be really, really deep.*

Both Qidira and I adored water, especially the ocean. We both loved to swim, but my troll genetics made me sink like a stone if I did not keep moving. River trolls are fairly heavy, so they can walk around on the bottom of a river or lake without floating up or being swept away by the current. They also have virtually impenetrable skin, and as far as I knew, they could hold their breath for almost an hour at a time. This allowed them to live in and around water, and go in and out without losing heat and moisture. I inherited my thick skin from that side of my family, but still, it was not as thick as full-blooded troll skin, and as I swam around, I felt the cold seep in. Soon, the sun dropped behind the trees and the valley was cast into shadow.

I looked back to the house in which we had settled and saw light dancing through the window. It spilled through the open door and flickered on the now matted grass, inviting me home. I swam back to where I could stand, climbed out, and quickly grabbed my clothes off of the stone table. Dripping lake water as I went, I hurried inside.

"Put these on," Qidira instructed as I stepped into the welcoming warmth. She handed me a long, thick shirt.

Next, she tossed me a matching pair of pants. I stripped off my wet underclothes and quickly re-dressed, savoring the warmth of my pajamas. She took my wet clothes and walked outside.

"Can you find me some spices or something?" she called over her shoulder. "Water itself won't fill us up enough to constitute dinner. I picked some orange yarrow root and mashed it up. It will add sweetness but find me something to go with it. Oh, and firewood, too, please." She laid my wet clothes on the table to dry and then came back inside. "I used what I could find to start the fire, but I would feel better if we could keep it alive through the night."

I put on my boots and left to gather seasoning for our supper. I found scattered sprigs of mint and a stand of licorice bark and thought that would have to suffice. On my way back, I went through a few of the larger houses, one of which even had a second story. Each home was in different stages of decay and disarray, but I found enough dry wood from old furniture to keep the fire alive until morning. During my search, I kept my eyes and ears open for any hint of life or a spot of evidence that we had indeed been followed; the trees rustled slightly, but I didn't see or hear anything that worried me.

We ate an odd but delicious stew and gobbled down berries I found for dessert. We shut the door before bed, and I moved the table in front of it just in case.

"It opens outwards," Qidira said flatly from her bed.

"Thank you, wise one. I know that, but if someone does come in, we'll at least have some forewarning as they run into the table."

"Ah," she said, humoring me. She lay down and pulled the blankets up to her chin.

I climbed under my own blankets and turned to face

her, propping my head up with one hand. "Weird day, huh?"

"Yes." She stared at the firelight dancing on the ceiling.

I dropped my head, resting one cheek against my forearm. "How are you doing, honey?"

She continued to stare at the ceiling. "I'm sad and scared. But mostly I'm sad." She said this matter-of-factly but her tone was gentle and I knew that being here triggered an emotional wrestling match inside of her. "I miss them both. I miss them so much it feels like my heart breaks every day. And now Strom. . ." Her voice cracked and she closed her eyes.

I sat up and pulled her into a hug. "I know the feeling."

She cried into my shoulder. When the sobs slowed and her breathing was less ragged, I let her go. She sat up next to me, wiping her face with both hands. I reached over and tucked a loose jet-black curl behind her ear.

"I'm so sorry," I said.

"I know. Thank you."

I was afraid to ask my next question, but I wanted to know for sure where her head was. "Are you worried that we will find Amil and Tariq?"

She nodded. "I don't know what I would do if I saw either of them again. When you want something so badly for so long, the possibility of it actually happening is . . ."

I finished her sentence for her. "Scary."

She nodded again and her shoulders heaved with a fresh wave of tears. Soon, however, fatigue took over, and we both settled in for the night.

"Elon, I love you. Thank you for being my family."

"I can't imagine it being any other way."

THE WAY IN

I slept with my normal warm feeling of familiarity, but no one visited me in my dreams. When I woke in the morning, Qidira was gone. Out in the dew-covered grass, I saw her little footprints leading to the bridge, and I looked over to find her standing over the stone trough. I slipped on my boots and rushed to her side.

She was muttering under her breath and did not notice my arrival.

"Couldn't stay away, huh?" I quipped.

She slapped the back of her hand against my arm but continued her mumbling. Soon, however, she took a breath and looked at me. "You're obnoxious."

"I know."

She glared at me with pursed lips. "It's not affecting me anymore. Before I came over, I said a spell my father taught me as a child. I used to use it to block my mother's dwarfen magic. It made her crazy."

"Sounds like something you would do."

She ignored me and continued, "It seems to have worked. And look at this . . ." She picked up a cup of water she brought with her and poured it into the stone trough. The liquid splashed and ran toward each end as you would expect, but once it reached its balance point something happened. It began sinking into the stone, and within seconds it was gone.

"I wondered . . . so I tried it with dirt and then leaves. They all disappeared as if they just soaked right through the basin." Her face was somber. "I don't know what this thing is."

"Did you figure out what the words mean?"

She nodded. "It says: 'To find Truth you must become bare and stand in the rain and the wind, and not shrink away from whatever they bring.'"

"What?"

"That, I can almost guarantee you, is not dwarfish. There are a lot of things we are, but poetic is not one of them."

"That's poetic?" Again, she slapped my arm with the back of her hand. "Seriously, any idea what it means?"

"The word Truth is capitalized and rain and wind are written larger than the rest of the words. It could be just a religious parable or something, or—"

"A ceremonial way to make me crazy?"

She stamped one foot and made an exasperated sound. "You asked. Stop being obnoxious, Gods. Did you drink obnoxious juice this morning? Stop and eat the obnoxious plant?"

I smiled. "Okay, okay, I promise, I'll stop. I'm just feeling particularly refreshed this morning." My mind still reeled and my heart ached from the events of the prior few days, but our night in the first settlement had renewed my sense of purpose.

We stood contemplating what the words might mean. Then, we walked along the shore of the lake, stopping at the black scar of the firepit. The ashes were old, sodden with years of rain. Rivulets had run through the dust, creating gouges in the residue that looked like veins. Still, nothing grew.

"What do you think happened here?" Qidira's voice was measured.

I had a feeling in my gut but could not put it into words. I shook my head. "I don't know."

In spite of the bright, morning sun, Qidira shivered. "Let's keep going."

We continued along the shore and when we got to the waterfall, mist blanketed us with fine dew and the power of the falling water pushed against us like a strong wind. In a simultaneous movement, we turned to each other.

"You think . . .?" I asked.

"It makes sense, it's wind and water," she replied.

We moved toward the tree line, where the bare rock of the mountain stood between the rising forest and the water. I pressed myself against the wall to peer behind the falls. There, a narrow stone ledge traveled along the cliff face, but I could not see a cave or a door or anything.

"I see a ledge but nothing else. Should we go in?"

"You first, you're the river troll."

I moved toward the water, but she grabbed my arm.

"Your clothes," she said. "It said you had to become bare."

"Are you kidding me?"

"No, really, I can only assume that means you gotta get nekked." She chortled.

I pulled off my clothes and started back toward the waterfall.

The mist was cool against my skin. Carefully, I put one foot onto the ledge behind the water. The rock was slippery, and I was surprised to find that it was warm. I pressed my back against the uneven rock face and edged toward the center. Chancing a look back at Qidira, I could just make out her watching me through the falling water.

As I neared the center of the ledge, all I heard was the rushing of the water as it fell past my face. The force of the waterfall now pressed me back against the rock. It took me a few more breaths to slide my way to what I thought was the center of the ledge. I lost sight of Qidira and my ears echoed with the whooshing sound of falling water.

Okay, I thought. *What now?*

I closed my eyes because it felt like the thing to do. I felt too vulnerable, so I opened them again. When I did, it was in time to see a streak of color zoom through the water inches from my nose. I was starting to think I made it up when I saw another one, and then two more. The blurs came more frequently until the curtain of water in front of me was a mosaic of moving color.

Then, all of a sudden, something nipped my toes. I looked down and saw a swarm of color around my feet. It began moving up my legs. Whatever they were, they bit me, repeatedly. When they stopped for a nibble, I caught a glimpse of the tiny creatures, who had scaly bodies of various colors adorned with clear, iridescent wings. I swatted at them; I kicked my legs out, attempting to shoo them away. Still, they climbed my body. I panicked, scared what might happen if they reached my face.

I moved back the way I came in an effort to escape the colorful barrage of little teeth. When I got a few steps away, the attack stopped, but they did not leave. Some of them landed on the ledge and began grooming themselves. Others hovered around their brethren, watching me. I stood for a couple of breaths, not sure what to do next. I recalled what the basin said: "and not shrink away from whatever they bring you." Was this some kind of annoying test? Reluctantly, I moved back toward the watery insects.

As I was about to re-enter their attack zone, a voice sounded from far away. I looked back and saw Qidira edging her way toward me. Her face was worried and she repeatedly looked over her shoulder. I strained to see past her and saw the cause of her anxiety. Near the opening to the waterfall stood small brown creatures that looked like fleshy tree stumps with arms and legs. They were attempting to come in under the water but seemed to dislike the prospect. One put a foot out and then pulled it back. There were three of them and they looked like they were pushing each other, trying to convince the others they should be the one to go after Qidira. I looked back and she mouthed, "Forest trolls."

She crept closer to me and her pursuers seemed to give up. I had never met a forest troll, so I did not know anything about them except what I had read as a child. From what I could remember, they were small, nasty creatures that lived in forests. They hid among the trees and could very convincingly make themselves appear to be part of the scenery, which was how they snagged whatever prey they got. They did not historically bother humans, which was probably why I had not seen them since my arrival on Palus. Still, I was sure Qidira would make a fine snack for their tribe.

Our aggressors scrutinized us with beetle black eyes as Qidira reached my side. She was fully clothed still, and her skirts were quickly becoming heavy with the mist that blanketed us both.

She took my hand and raised her voice so I could hear her. "They came out of the forest a few breaths after you came in. There is a whole gang of them out there; at least fifteen or twenty, like little sticks banging around at my legs, ripping at my clothes. They tried to pull me to the ground. When one jumped on my back, I decided it was time to follow you. I got in a few good kicks and even sent some scurrying back into the forest, but there were just too many of them."

I motioned toward the creepy swarm of flying biters.

Qidira's eyebrows shot up and she rolled her eyes. "Water sprites. They're harmless but can be annoying if they get worked up. What's going on?"

I told her what happened as best as I could over the roar of water, ending with my thoughts about this being some kind of test. The corners of her mouth turned down as she contemplated the information.

"Shall we?" she asked.

"Sure, but you're still clothed," I pointed out. "I think you have to take your clothes off, too."

Careful to watch my footing, I helped her undress. She let her garments slip off the stone, to be carried off to the depths of the lake. Her face registered annoyance at losing her clothing. Holding hands, we moved to the middle of the ledge, our backsides scraping against the rough rock-face. As soon as we got there, the sprites started biting me again. It was annoying, like tiny pin pricks all over my skin. When they reached my hips, they moved to the left side of my body, away from Qidira. I looked over and saw her watching them, yet none of them touched her. She shrugged and shook her head as if to say that she did not know what was going on either.

The sprites continued up my torso. When they reached my face and began scratching at my closed eyelids, it was all I could do not to bat at them. Before they could start in on my mouth, I rolled my lips in between my teeth; I knew they would not break my skin anywhere else but there. Still, it was maddening nonetheless. Buzzing filled my left ear as they worked that skin over, too, but soon, the noise ended. I opened my eyes and watched as they zoomed back into the falling water and down into the lake.

Pulling in deep breaths, I looked at Qidira.

She leaned over and said, close to my ear, "You're lucky your skin is thick. They can leave a human quite bloody."

"Why didn't they bite you?"

She shook her head again. "I don't know."

Before we had time to say anything else, something heavy and coarse grabbed one of my ankles. I let out an involuntary shriek, which was swallowed by the continuously cascading water. I looked down and saw a dark gray, leathery hand wrapped around my left ankle. It started pulling me down. The hand was strong as it tried to drag me off of the stone shelf. Instinctively, I pulled back against the force. I knew what I was looking at; the skin was familiar. A river troll was trying to pull me into the water.

"Qid, help!" I fought as hard as I could, but I knew that I would not be able to hold on for much longer.

"Stop fighting," she commanded.

"Are you insane? That's a full-blooded river troll right there. If I stop fighting, I'll be dragged to the depths of this creepy lake." I gripped the wet rock as best as I could, pressing my head against the uneven surface.

"Look, I know it is your nature to fight, but try, for once, not to. Close your eyes and stand as still as you can."

I glared at her, narrowing my eyes. But, following her direction, I stopped struggling as best as I could. Soon, the traction on my ankle lessened. Still, however, the troll maintained its grip on my leg.

"Completely, Elon. Stop fighting, completely. Damn it,

listen to me, you crazy half-breed!" I saw the look of fear in her eyes and let go of my belligerence.

I turned my face back to the water, closed my eyes, and sucked in a deep, humid breath. Amazingly, the troll loosened its grip. I took in another deep breath and focused on quieting all of my muscles. I became conscious of how my feet felt on the rock, how the troll's skin felt against mine; I felt my backside pressed against the ragged cliff face, and I noticed that my left hand was still holding on as hard as it could to the stone next to me.

I loosened my grip and dropped my hand to my side. At the same time, I moved my attention to my right hand and felt it clinging to Qidira. I loosened that, too, and brought that arm down to my side as well. I took in a third deep breath. At the end of my exhalation, I opened my eyes as the troll's hand slowly slid from my foot. I watched the gray fingers disappear back into the water. Qidira smiled. It was a characteristically proud smile, and for the second time in three days, I wanted to poke her in her eyes.

"Good job. Thank you for listening. For a moment I thought he might actually get you . . . and then I would have had to come in after you, and while I am an okay swimmer, I sure could not beat a full-blooded river troll . . . and it would have been all over for both of us." She smiled and rested her body back against the slick rock behind us. She leaned her head back, still smiling.

Without warning, she began sinking into the rock. As if the stone liquified, her body moved *into* the rock. It happened quickly and by the time I grabbed her hand with both of mine all that was left in the open were her forearms, and those were quickly swallowed up as well. Now facing the rock, her fingers slipped through mine and my hand hit solid rock. I desperately felt the hard, jagged surface for a door or trigger. My fingers scraped at imagined cervices; I pounded on the stone, kicking it as if I could break through.

I panicked. I had to find Qidira. The thought of her flowed through my brain as I turned to face the waterfall once more. I pressed as much of myself against the rock as I could, desperately trying to focus on what was written on the stone basin.

Don't fight, don't fight, I repeated to myself.

No sooner had I closed my eyes then something grabbed both of my ankles. My feet started slipping out from under me as the troll pulled me toward the water and it took everything I had to give over to it. I focused all of my concentration on relaxing and letting it happen. As I fell onto my backside, and my feet touched the water, two things happened at the same time: the troll let go and my head and arms sunk into the rock.

Unlike when Qidira disappeared, my transition through the rough surface seemed to happen in slow motion. I felt as though something was dragging me through a crushing mound of gravel. The rock scraped my face and hands. I could not open my eyes, nor could I breathe. Soon I felt my legs and feet enter the mountain wall as well.

I had a moment to reflect, and I thought, *through the rock . . . huh. Couldn't have been around it, or over it, or even a magic door, it had to be* through *the rock.* As my body continued to endure the crushing trip, and my chest was unable to expand, I realized I had other things to worry about. Not being able to breath might cause a problem.

My body utilized oxygen at a slower rate. My cells somehow cleaned the carbon dioxide and reused the oxygen. This meant I could hold my breath for longer than normal periods of time, something the trolls used while hunting underwater. After a while, however, even that failed me and my lungs started to burn. I tried to breathe, but my chest could not expand.

I needed this to end; I needed to get to wherever I was going. The process was agonizing and I felt like the rock scraping against my skin would persist until I died. My head spun. My fingers and toes started to tingle and white spots flashed on the backs of my eyelids as the oxygen in my blood ran out. I was suffocating.

Just as I was starting to reflect that this might be the way I died—traveling through magic rock—I burst free and my chest involuntarily expanded. My eyes flew open as I fell forward, plummeting toward the ground. As I made contact with a stone floor, something cracked in my right knee. I rolled onto my side and then rocked over onto my back, cradling my broken kneecap. I heard myself saying, in between gasps of air, "Ow, ow, ow . . ." After I rolled around for about ten breaths my eyes finally focused on where I was.

DWARFS

*J*t was dark. Shadows danced on stone walls and a low, stone ceiling. My brain processed the information, telling me that there must be a fire nearby. I tipped my head back further and had a quick upside-down glance at three men standing behind me.

I flipped over as rapidly as I could and tried to scramble to my feet. A hot streak of pain drove me to the ground again and I grasped my knee where I felt the bone broken below my skin. Catching my breath, I looked up to see the three small men standing in front of me. Qidira stood to my left with a blanket around her shoulders, and looking from her to the men I saw that they were at least a foot shorter than she. Seeing the blanket reminded me that I was naked, and as I looked down, I reflexively drew my legs up to my abdomen. A small female hurried from behind the men and brought me a blanket similar to the one Qidira wore. I wound it around my shoulders and back and sneezed.

"Dwarfs?" I directed this question at Qidira, rubbing my nose.

"Uh, Elon . . ." She looked toward the men, who did not appear happy.

The littlest of the three stood in front of the other two. His arms were folded across his chest and his strong face was set in a scowl. He had a wide, defined jawline and deep eyes that looked black from this distance. I noticed his beautifully crafted leather boots, which looked perfect with the deep green velvet clothes he wore. Threads of gold wound through the fabric and there was an intricate crest embroidered over his left breast. An ornately carved silver sword hung from his waist.

I turned my attention to his companions, who both had their swords drawn, points in the ground in front of them, hands folded on the butt of the hilt. Both of them wore the same velvet fabric but theirs was less vibrant, and there were no embellishments. They were looking at me with interest, but not the oh-I'd-like-to-get-to-know-her kind of interest. It was more like the confident I-will-kill-you-if-I-have-to, just-try-me kind of interest.

The dwarf in front spoke. "Yes, we are dwarfs. And we can answer our own questions. You are Elon, no? The Sidar told us to expect you, but do not think we are happy about it." His face softened as he looked toward Qidira. "I must say, however, that I was not expecting this one." He executed a small bow in her direction. "*You* I know, although I have not seen you in quite a few moons." His voice held an elegant brogue, which caused everything he said to sound romantic, even his angry words aimed at me.

I looked to Qidira, who gave me a look that said, *let me do this.*

"Sir," she said, bowing deeper toward him than he had toward her, "thank you for allowing us to enter your domain. Also, I thank you for bringing my friend in even though I know you have reservations." I was impressed with her tone of voice. Even I believed her obsequious countenance.

The man in charge strolled to her. She remained in her bow and, even bent over, she was still taller than he was. He placed a hand under her chin and raised her face. She stood to her full height, her face flirtatious, almost rapturous. I thought I was going to be ill.

"Qidira." Excitement tinged his voice.

A look of confusion flashed across her face so quickly that I am not sure he saw it. She closed and opened her eyes slowly as an indication of confirmation. Not that he had said her name with any doubt; he seemed to know just who she was.

"I am so glad that you came to see us, finally. I watched you when you lived out there, with your child, but you chose to go down the mountain instead of into it. You enchant me more now then you did then."

Qidira hesitated before she curtsied. Her face was composed, but her lips were drawn tighter and I could tell she had heartache and anger roiling in her heart. Still, I saw that the compliment was not lost on her.

I watched the interaction with great interest. It seemed amazing to me that three days ago I did not even know there were dwarfs on this planet and now I was sitting in some dwarfish habitat. I looked around again. We were in a solid cave, made entirely of rock. The only way out was a tunnel behind the men who still stood in front of me with their swords drawn. I turned and stared at the wall behind me, to see if our traverse left any sign. It had not. I heard my name and quickly turned back.

"What? I mean, yes, uh, sir?" I was trying to follow Qidira's lead. The simpering approach did not work as well for me. Or perhaps it was that I was not as adept at carrying it off. Either way, one side of the little man's mouth twitched. He grunted almost inaudibly and stared at me for at least three breaths before offering me his hand. I took it, and, holding onto the blanket covering my nakedness, I gingerly got to my feet. My knee hurt, but it had already started healing, so the pain was less the sharp agony of an acute injury and more the dull ache of rebuilding.

Qidira hugged me. "You okay?" she whispered. "How's your knee?"

"Healing," I responded quietly. "What's up, princess? What's with the adoration?"

She squeezed my arm and issued a small *tisk*. "It freaks me out that this dwarf knows who I am, and it freaks me out even more that he watched me all those years ago. I mean, that's just creepy." I nodded. Her expression changed, and I heard good old Qidira come out. "But what can I say?"

The man behind us cleared his throat. He was standing once more in front of his two sentries. He addressed his next speech to both of us.

"I am Aarick, son of Aarron, who is the son of Aadrick." He uttered these words as if they would mean something to us. When we did not respond, he continued, "Welcome to Truth, the home of the original inhabitants of this world and the seat of the great knowledge of the dwarfs. We welcome those who seek justice, balance, and home. We will not tolerate murder or treachery. Any wrongs committed against the people of this place will be punishable by high expulsion into the deep waters on the other side of that wall." He pointed toward the solid stone behind us. I reflexively looked over my shoulder and back again.

I whispered out of the side of my mouth, "High expulsion? As opposed to low expulsion?"

Qidira replied, "I think they throw you over the edge of somewhere high up."

"Ah," I said. Once again, Aarick's sneer chastised me. "Sorry." My curiosity subdued my annoyance.

The small man continued, "If you will follow us, we will find a temporary place for you. Once you are fully healed, rested, and well fed, we will help you find the Sidar."

I shot a questioning look at Qidira. She shrugged and shook her head at the same time, as if telling me, *I don't know and don't you dare ask him.*

"Vamphyre, I must warn you that blood-letting, even if the victim survives, is strictly prohibited here. Do not even think about feeding on anyone, or I will kill you myself."

"Uhm . . ." I looked at Qidira. "No worries from me. Qid, what about you?" She pinched my thigh.

He continued to glare at me with warning. "Follow me, then. Vamphyre, these two will help you if you need it." He indicated the men with the weapons.

"Thank you," I said, trying, successfully I thought, to imbue my words with the sound of true gratitude. "I believe I'll be okay."

"Well, then." He gestured to the female and she handed us two thick, long white shirts, which, once adorned, hung to Qidira's feet and my thighs. When we were done dressing, the female whispered something, and Aarick turned to leave; she fell into step behind him. The guards waited for us to go before bringing up the rear.

My gait was slower than normal due to my injury, but the limp actually kept me at the pace of our leader. I leaned into Qidira, who had one arm around my waist and one on my arm. I assumed this was to make sure I did not fall. Either that or she wanted to have a good grip in case she needed to control me.

"Does he have to keep calling me 'vamphyre'? I mean, there are three other parts of me he could choose from." I tried to keep my voice down so it would not reach Aarick, son of Aaron, son of Aadrick.

"I guess the vamphyre is the only part of you that is dangerous to them."

"What, river trolls are welcome visitors here?"

"I don't know, maybe. That one in the lake has to work with them in order for the test to work, so perhaps they are friendly with the trolls."

"Unless it was more magic."

"Hmm, possibly." Her voice dropped lower, and she said, "Elon, I think you have figured out that they did not want to let you through the rock."

"But I passed their annoying test."

"But you are part vamphyre."

"Enough already with the vamphyre, I get it. So, what made them bring me through?"

"Well, the Sidar are looking for you, are they not? And since the dwarfs and the Sidar have been working together for some reason . . . I guess they did as they were told? Plus, I begged them to. I added tears and I think that was a nice touch; I know it worked on Aarick. I also told them that if they didn't trust you once they got to know you, they could kill you."

I stopped and said, my voice heavy with disbelief, "Did you really tell them they could kill me?"

Qidira kept walking with her head held high and said over her shoulder, "Yup. Now come on."

I limped as quickly as I could to catch up with her.

TRUTH

$\mathcal{W}$e wound through rocky tunnels, and I tried to remember the way we had come: left, then right, then left . . . but after a while, I lost track. Somewhere up ahead, the sound of running water echoed off of high walls. Soon, the dirt floor sloped upwards until we were standing at a flat wooden bridge.

The bridge spanned a small underground river that ran along the side wall of a cavernous room. The river came out through a small opening in the left side, flowed under the bridge, and disappeared under the opposite wall. The water was a swirling azure, with shifting whirls of blue that melted into a smoky green near the edges. It was entrancing and made me want to walk into it fully clothed. I felt a small hand on my back and realized I had stopped in the middle of the bridge, and the dwarfs behind me were directing me to continue forward.

As we crossed, I had a full view of the cavern and my mouth fell open. I gaped at the immense space in which we found ourselves. The floor swam with shadows of shifting green light. I looked up and saw water shimmering above us. Nothing seemed to be keeping it from falling into the room and I had a moment of panic as I thought about what a sudden rush of water would do to us in this cavern. I gazed at Qidira, and she looked at me, her mouth partially open as well.

Aarick watched us with a gratified smile and after noting our reaction he simply said, "Magic."

He motioned to his guards who bowed and disappeared through a hole in the wall to our right. As the velvet curtain covering their exit fell closed, I glimpsed small downward leading stairs. Directly in front of us, across the length of the cavern, was a wide arch that reached halfway to the water above us. Stairs leading upwards spanned the width of the gap. To the left of the stairs was a small door, a dwarf-sized door, made of plain wood. It stood out because, of all the openings in the hall, this was the only plain door, and it was much smaller than the others.

As we stepped deeper into the room, I got a better view of the large, circular opening on the left-hand wall. I peered through the aperture and saw another, smaller room similar to the one we were in.

To our right, next to the curtained tunnel our guards used, two large stone projections flanked an elaborately carved wooden double door. The stone structures started where the floor met the wall and angled up and out. Swirls of orange-brown and white danced through the stone, which rose in differently shaped fingers, to various heights. The result was a scallop shell appearance. At the base of each of these monuments was a hole and carved down into the wall of the rock was a ladder.

I turned my attention to the door. The engraving in the wood, which split in half when the door opened, was the same crest Aarick wore on his shirt. *Maybe he is some kind of little king*, I thought, slowly walking to the center of the cavern.

My eyes drank in the smooth walls, which were made up of layers of different types of material. Lines of sediment, granite, limestone, and marble glistened in the shifting light. It was as if someone carved a cross section through the mountain and then polished it. The layered edges of the room seemed alive as they sloped up and inwards toward the water, leaving the room with the feeling of a deep fishbowl.

The floor was as smooth as the walls, made of dark marble. The veins of the rock spun across the room following no particular pattern, pulling the eye to follow their haphazard journey. Whorls of whites, blacks, dark blues, and gold reflected the movement of the water above.

Soon, I found myself in the center of the main cavern. Looking down, I saw a mosaic, a water scene encircled in gold. Turtles, fish, plants, snakes, shells, and what I now knew were water sprites all swam around four spheres. The center sphere was made of a shimmering rock I could not identify, and three smaller globes were set evenly around it. All of the images were carved out of different stones and set flawlessly into the granite. The wings of the sprites shifted colors and I recognized them as white opal, a gem I had only read about. I looked closer and saw that the bodies were made from malachite, hematite, and lapis. Around the circle, the swirling granite continued as if the carvings had been there since the birth of the mountain.

"Qidira, look at this." I pulled her over until we both had a view of the design. "Does that look familiar?"

Comprehension dawned in her eyes. "Of course. The Sidar . . . Strom, our roof, now here . . ." She looked up into my face. "Elon, what's going on?"

"I don't know."

Qidira and I walked slowly around and over the mosaic, enjoying the textures and colors yet contemplating what connection Strom may have had with the dwarfs, or the Sidar. When we were done, Aarick led us to the left, through the circular opening, and into the smaller cavern.

The walls of the smaller space were different from the one we had just left. Along the dull, jagged back wall of the room, stairs disappeared into the rock at various heights. Large sections of stone jutted out at all angles, to different lengths. The light in this cavern came from not one but multiple small holes in the stone ceiling.

The same stunning water we crossed to enter the big room ran along the left side of this room as well, disappearing under the wall and into the main cavern. The right side looked like there had been a cave-in, with boulders and stones scattered along the ground, in an immense pile against the wall. If it was indeed the vestiges of a natural occurrence, the dwarves had capitalized on it. Carved into the boulders were countless seats and tables, at which dwarfs were seated, enjoying food and conversation.

Aarick turned to the dwarf woman who was still with us and whispered something. To us, he said, "Tisa will help you get settled. She will bring you your clothes and anything else you might need. Your belongings have already been brought through and placed in a room for you." His hand motioned toward the wall full of stairs.

Tisa led us into the rock. We climbed in semi-darkness until the stairs opened into a circular room with high walls. In the middle of the wall to my left was an opening, just big enough for one person to walk through. It was the only egress other than the one through which we had just emerged.

The ceiling was open, with the magic water shimmering green light down on us. On the floor was an exquisitely woven rug of cream, blue, gold, and green. It reminded me of the carpet in our loft at home. Gazing around, I saw two thick white cushions on either side of the round space with smaller pillows of greens and blues set in a row against the wall, and at the back was a small wooden table with two chairs. At my waist level, niches were cut into the rock at various intervals. Our traveling gear was piled at the doorway; it looked old and worn next to our surroundings. Immediately, I noticed that my knife was missing.

"I will return with food. Please, use the bathroom to freshen up." Tisa motioned towards the other, smaller doorway. Then, indicating two niches in the wall, she said, "There are clothes there for you." She clasped her hands together and looked at us. "Do you need anything else right now?"

We both shook our heads.

"No, thank you," I said.

"Thank you, Tisa," Qidira said, and the little woman left with a backward glance.

I looked down the steps after her and when the sound of her footfalls disappeared, I said, "Okay Qidira, this is both really cool and really freaking me out."

"Me, too."

She moved to a pile of clothes. Picking up the top item, she unfolded it and held it out in front of her. It was similar to what we were wearing now: off-white, natural fiber that was exceptionally soft and warm.

"Wool," she said. "I'm betting mountain goat wool, the under-belly hair. I have never seen the actual goat, but I have seen this fabric before. The Sidar used to wear it." She pressed her nose against the material as if some scent would be there to comfort her.

I went to check out the bathroom. It was a miniature

version of our main bedroom except in the back there was a commode and against another wall a basin rested on a wooden stand with a tap coming out of the wall. I looked down into the commode. It was a long, deep, dark hole.

Fantastic, I thought. *This mountain is sitting on one giant latrine.*

I moved to the sink and turned on the tap. Icy water flowed into the basin. A ring hung on the wall as well and when I pulled it the bottom of the basin slid to the side. I watched as he water fell down the hollow wooden stand and disappeared into another dark hole. I turned off the water and returned to the main room.

Qidira had started unpacking our gear, and she was now wearing the dwarf-made pajamas. She had taken down her hair and the black curls hung wildly against the white of her new garments. Her back was to me and she was folding my clothes on what I assumed was going to be my bed.

"A for real bathroom," I said.

When I reached her side, I saw that she was crying. I knew she was folding clothes, being domestic, caring for me, in an effort to keep herself busy. I sat at the table and, lacing my fingers together on the top of my head, I released air slowly through pursed lips. I was overwhelmed, and I knew Qidira was, too. If we had to be here, underground, I was glad it was here in this small hole in the rock away from everyone else. We both needed food, sleep, and privacy.

As I was thinking of breaking the silence, Tisa knocked on the wall down a few steps. It was not a real knock, more of a dull thudding noise, but it worked to let us know she was there. Qidira relieved Tisa of her tray as she entered the room and carried it to the table.

On the tray was an oil lamp with a round, ceramic

base. The wick was protected by a cylinder of clear, hand-blown glass. Air bubbles dotted the glass, left by the artisan who created the piece. When Tisa lit the beige wick, the fire played with the imperfections and light danced on the walls. Tisa stood in the doorway and asked again if we needed anything.

"Actually, yeah," I said, sitting forward. "Can you tell me something about where we are?"

She looked over her shoulder and then back to us, as if she was afraid Aarick, son of Aarron, and so forth, would dash up behind her and chastise her for fraternizing. Qidira and I glanced at each other, waiting to see how she would react to the question.

What she did next surprised us. Her stance changed: she held her head higher, pushed her shoulders back, and placed her hands at her side. Again, Qidira and I looked at each other, trying to read the body language. I wanted to laugh because the silence was killing me. Qidira just turned patient eyes to the small woman.

Tisa wore a simple dress made from heavy cotton that had been dyed crimson. It had a square neckline that exposed her collar bones. The sleeves gathered at the shoulder before spilling down the arms, narrowing at the wrists. The skirts almost touched the ground, and she was wearing leather moccasins. Her hair was black, and the front was pulled into a small bun at the back of her head while the rest had been braided and wrapped back up around the bun. Delicate curls framed her light brown face and I noticed that her eyes were not just black, but eddied with swirls of gray, like smoke curling inside dark a marble.

"Aarick told you where you are," she finally said.

"Yes," I quickly replied. "But I don't actually know what that means."

"Are you really part vamphyre?" The question caught me off guard.

"Uh, yeah, you can't tell? I thought all you people had, like, a vampy sense that tingled when one of us got near." I did not bother to hide my sarcasm or annoyance.

"All of *us people* aren't pure dwarf. Like her." She pointed to Qidira, whose eyebrows shot up as if to say, *Why are you bringing me into this?*

But Tisa's attention was now on Qidira, which was fine with me because I was done with talking about being a vamphyre. She continued, "We have magic because we are dwarfs, but the rest of our abilities depend on what other kinds of wood make up our family tree." She was still staring intently at Qidira. "I am part troll"—she looked at me— "like you. Only, my great-grandfather was a forest troll." She looked back to Qidira. "My magic is good for hiding, and for luring people to me." I felt a slight pull in her direction.

"Funny," I said, "and definitely cool magic, but don't do that again."

"Sorry," she said, but I could tell her apology was not sincere.

"Okay," I responded, "so not everyone here is pure dwarf . . . what's the story with Aarick and his father of his father of his father?"

She kept her eyes on Qidira as she answered me. "He is the third grandson of the current king, Aadrick. Aadrick has been alive for five hundred years now"—Qidira shot me an impressed look— "and will be resigning the crown to his son, Aarron, when the snow comes."

"Wow, so, like, we got the royal treatment, for real, huh?" I chuckled at my own joke. Sometimes I think I am funny, and sometimes I am, but sometimes I only make myself laugh. That was good enough for me in most circumstances, but I remembered that this young woman standing in front of me might not be in the mood for jokes. Qidira saved me.

"Tisa, is that why you are the one escorting us? Because you are also Other?"

"Yes," she replied. "But I volunteered to greet you, too." The smoke in her eyes flared. "We knew you were here. Yesterday, when you touched the stone, we knew there was a fairy nearby. Then you sent through the water and the forest debris . . . we knew you would figure it out. When we saw you move toward the water this morning, Aarick was sent to bring you through, and I volunteered to go with him."

We both seemed to have missed the last few sentences.

"Wait, go back to the fairy thing?" I sat on the edge of my seat, feet planted firmly on the rock.

"You, the fairy." She pointed at Qidira.

"Wait, wait, what? She's not. . . But sometimes I've wondered. . ." I turned toward Qidira to see if she had anything to add.

She stared back at me with surprise, and when she looked at Tisa it seemed as if she was unable to get her words out as fast as they were forming in her head. Finally, she said, "Excuse me?"

"Please don't try to tell me," Tisa answered with indignation, "that you don't know you have fairy blood. I saw the magic you performed out there." She looked like she thought we were having a joke at her expense.

"No, really, I don't think she knows what you're talking about." I turned to Qidira, and said, "I mean . . . do you?"

Qidira shook her head.

Tisa blinked at us in disbelief. "You never noticed how things seemed to grow around you? How flowers are stronger, fruits more plentiful, and animals more robust?"

She leaned toward Qidira. "Didn't you ever notice that when people are around you, *they seem more alive?*" Her voice rang with reverence.

Qidira contemplated the floor, the beds, the lamp, and finally the water above us. "No, I did not notice," she finally replied.

"I did," I added

"And so did you," Tisa said to Qidira. "I can see it in your face."

All of sudden it seemed that whatever held Tisa back released and she rushed across the room to sit on the edge of the cushion closest to Qidira's chair. She leaned forward, beaming with child-like anticipation.

"Madame Qidira, you are the reason we can survive here. Your people blessed us with fairy magic and we have reaped the rewards ever since." She gestured at the ceiling. "When you left the settlement out there it was decided to put the stone trough next to the lake in case you returned. The stone would suck a fairy in, make it drunk with magic. And it worked, didn't it?"

"Yes." Qidira looked squarely at the young dwarf in front of her. She tipped her head to one side, and then the other. Finally, she said, "I always just thought I was special, that the Gods had given me gifts."

Tisa beamed. "She did give you gifts. The rare genetic gift of a fairy somewhere in your bloodline." I thought the girl was going to burst with excitement. "And here you are —a *dwarf* with fairy blood. There is only one Other here who has that specific gift." She looked sidewise at us, anxiety lining her young face. I did not think Qidira noticed; she was lost in thought, staring at something across the room. I followed her gaze and all I saw was the wall. I did not interrupt her reverie.

I waved my hands around in front of me as if I could

clear the fog from my head with that simple motion. "Wait, wait, this is too much for me. I don't know any fairies"—I looked at Qidira— "well, I guess I do. Wow . . . this explains tons." I stood up and paced the room. I quickly remembered that Qidira was probably having feelings about this, too, so I moved back to the table and sat across from her, taking her hands in mine.

"Qidira, honey? Are you okay?" I asked.

"Yes."

"Really, because I gotta say, I'm not getting a lot of *okay* coming from you right now."

She looked from me to Tisa and back again. A smile crept across her face and I saw her eyes light up. "I love it. I love it!" It was her turn to stand up and flit around the space. She raised her hands to the water and said, "That is so cool. And those were my people!" She brought her hands back down and placed them on her hips. "This does explain a lot, doesn't it?" She kneeled in front of Tisa. "So, there are others still, yes?"

"Not many, and there are no full-blooded fairies left on Palus. But yes, we know of at least one more like you." Tisa fidgeted.

I saw where this was going and I figured tonight was not the night, that Qidira might face this better after some sleep. I did something I had only done twice to Qidira in the past. While each of those instances had been accidental, this time was intentional. I used what little vamphyre mind control I had and invaded her mind.

I do not have the full power to control another's mind. I cannot creep in and direct people against their will. My power is diluted and elusive. I can only strongly suggest ideas. In this case, I urged Qidira to end the conversation and pick it up in the morning.

Qidira's face went blank.

Soon, however, she stood up and, in one quick movement, turned on me and roared, "Did you just invade my mind?" Her eyes flared from their normal yellow-green to dark amber. Heat flared off of her and I stepped back. I attempted to set my face in a look of innocence, but instead, it registered my fear and surprise at the power radiating from her.

Tisa edged toward the door. "I will come back in the morning." She hurried away down the stairs. Neither of us paid attention to her words. We were too busy with our stand-off.

My skin bristled as the warmth became uncomfortable. The vamphyre part of me was afraid, as if she truly was made of fire and I would soon burn.

"Qidira . . ." I was lost for words. I saw her close her eyes and the heat retreated back into her.

We stood in silence for a charged moment.

"What the hell was that?" I asked, both in disbelief and with curiosity about this new power.

She blinked rapidly and when she looked back at me, her eyes were their normal color again. "What?"

"What was that? Your eyes, and the heat, and . . . what was that?"

"I don't know," she said. "But, wow, I feel wiped out." She sat down hard on the cushion behind her.

I joined her on the bed and kept my hands folded in my lap, scared to touch her lest I feel her fire once again. We both stared at the pattern on the rug. With a sigh, she leaned her head against my shoulder and I rested my head on hers.

"I cannot believe you were in my head. Don't think I'll forget about that, *vamphyre*." She sounded venomous, but I heard the undertone of joviality.

"I won't, I mean, I don't. I mean . . . I know what I did; I did it on purpose."

"That makes it even worse."

"I know."

We did not talk about it anymore. We sat with our heads together, holding hands until all of the light coming through the water was gone. Then we ate the meal Tisa had brought and fell asleep.

IGNACIA

*I*t did not take long for the Sidar to come to me that night. It was the same white-faced man as before, the elder. He was framed in smoky mist, and I could not see where he was or if there was anyone around him.

"Elon, thank you for coming." Unlike our prior encounters, this time, he spoke aloud. "I trust that our friends the dwarfs have treated you well so far." It was not a question. "I cannot come to you right now, none of us can. There is one who can lead you to us, however. You will know her when you see her, and she will know you. Sleep well, rest, take joy in your friends. Trust yourself, *and do not lose your way*. We look forward to seeing you." He disappeared.

I woke up and lay still, staring at the light from the lamp on the bottom of the water overhead. Leaving the warmth of my mattress, I went to the bathroom and drank water from the tap. It was cold and crisp and tasted cleaner than the water outside of the mountain. It swept away some of the fear from my throat. I turned and looked at myself in the mirror that hung above the sink.

My hair was down and disheveled, with parts of it clumping together like stiff bunches of hay. I would have to bathe in the morning. I looked at my face and was surprised to find comfort in my reflection. My mind chewed on the events of the last three days and realized I did not have any idea what was coming.

When I am fighting, I am driven by adrenaline and survival. When there is nothing going on, it is easy for me to be quiet and find my center; it is easier for me to return to who I am and spend time with myself. It is when I have to wait, or when things are unsure, that I find myself flailing for answers. It is when I am insecure and scared that I want someone to tell me what to do.

The minute the thought entered my mind, I tried to push it away. I hated when I felt that way. I saw it as a weakness. I closed my eyes and sighed.

Nothing ever goes away because I wish it to.

It was my experience, actually, that when I resisted internal change, the need for said change only became more pronounced. I was going to have to accept my fear. It was part of who I was. I was going to have to use it as we moved forward.

"The truth will set me free," I said to myself, "but first it might piss me off." This was something Qidira and I said often, especially when one of us was confronting a not-so-glamorous facet of our personalities. "And in this case, girlie," I continued to my reflection, "I'm fairly sure you are going to need all you've got, the good and the not-so-good, to fight this fight."

I got back into bed. Looking over at Qidira on her own mattress across the room, I saw her eyes moving behind her eyelids. *I hope she's dreaming sweet dreams*, I thought. I laid down and fell almost instantly back to sleep.

The rest of my night was filled with cloudy dreams about water and tunnels. I kept following flashes of light down one corridor, and then another . . . I wound endlessly through ever smaller tunnels, never catching the glowing spark. In the end, I was standing on the edge of a precipice, alone and cold, looking down at the marshes and forests of Palus.

I awoke when Qidira climbed into bed with me. I could tell she had been awake for a while because she had changed and her hair was braided down her back.

"I waited, Elon," she said sheepishly, "but I need some cuddling." She snuggled in next to me; I put my arms around her and hugged her. As the warmth of her small body brought me comfort, I realized I needed affection as well.

The sun shone brightly through the water and its reflections danced through the room. We lay in bed talking, reviewing what had happened over the last few days. Eventually, we arrived at the subject I attempted to avoid the prior evening.

"So, this fairy Other . . ." Qidira said.

There was a moment of silence before I answered.

"Yes . . .?" I murmured in gentle encouragement.

"Do you think he is here?" She turned toward me and leaned her cheek on her hand.

"I don't know, but I am pretty sure I know someone who could tell us." I got out of bed and moved toward our belongings.

I changed back into my own clothes and gathered my stiff hair into a bunch at the back of my head. I really was going to need to take a bath. I found my knife sheath and hung it around my waist. All of my weapons were missing, but I wanted to have a place to put it when I got my knife back. Qidira was out of bed, with shoes on, waiting for me when I was done. We headed down the stairs into the jagged-walled room.

As we emerged from our little hole in the rock, we saw Tisa striding toward us. "I'm glad you two are awake. Before we get started with a full tour and introductions, I'm assuming you all will want to clean up and eat, yes?"

Without waiting for a response, she ushered us toward the river at the edge of the room. When we were standing on the bank, we saw a ledge that led off to a small doorway in the rock face. She led us through this door and into a crevasse full of stalagmites and stalactites.

"Which ones point up? I can never remember," I said under my breath.

Qidira leaned in and responded, "Stalactites drop from the top. Get it? Stalac*t*ites, *t*op?"

"Right, of course."

At the apex of the back of the room, water fell from a natural fissure into a large, round pool worn in the rock. Out of that pool, the water fell to the side and into a similar, lower pool. This continued through at least five different levels until the water finally settled into a steaming body of water next to our feet. From there, it flowed out under the rock wall and into the next room.

A fine mist danced at the top of the water, just like in the marsh when the temperature of the water was greater than that of the air. I stuck my hand in the nearest pool. "It's warm. Nice."

"It's beautiful," Qidira said to Tisa with a smile.

In two of the pools, we saw female dwarfs bathing. Carefully carved steps led up to and sometimes around the pools to allow access. On flattened boulders next to us were stacks of towels and small glass bottles of different colored liquids. Tisa offered us each two bottles and a towel.

It took us a few tries to figure out what was in each flask, but finally, we were both clean. We sat and relaxed, watching the bubbles float over the waterfall. When we were done, I felt dirty re-dressing in my own clothes but donned the dirty garments anyway. While the dwarfs had provided us with fresh clothes, none of them were crafted for someone my size. I was not sure what was going to happen for the rest of this day, but I wanted to know I could move freely if needed.

Tisa was waiting for us when we climbed the few steps back into the jagged room. She smiled and led us toward the opposite end, where the remains of the cave-in were being used for good purpose. A waist-high rock had been flattened and polished, and two smaller stones sat next to it to serve as chairs. On the smooth surface, there was bread and fruit waiting for us. Glass goblets full of dark purple liquid accompanied the food and I realized how hungry I was. We sat down, said our blessing, and then tentatively tried a bite of everything on the table.

The bread was warm, and there was goat cheese that held a gentleness I had never tasted; the cheese we had in the marsh was often musky and harsh. The purple liquid turned out to be grape juice, which was sweeter and more satisfying than any juice I had tasted before. The fruit on the table was orange and tender, and when I bit into it, it cut like butter.

When we had eaten our full, we looked around for Tisa. We saw her standing next to the large circular opening that led into the smooth cavern we originally entered last night. She was talking to a blond male dwarf, who soon nodded at something she said and disappeared into the big room. We joined her.

"Was the meal satisfactory?" She looked at Qidira.

"Yes, actually, quite tasty," I asserted. She looked at me sidewise. I smiled, amused with my own belligerence. I could tell I was going to take a back seat today.

"Do you feel ready to meet the royal family?" Tisa asked.

"Sure," Qidira answered, and then asked me, "you?"

"Sure." I nudged her with the toe of my boot. "Anything you want to ask . . .?"

"Um, yeah." She faced Tisa. "When might I meet this remaining fairy Other?"

"Of course," Tisa answered after a moment of hesitation. "Hopefully you will have a chance, um, soon. However, right now we need to meet with Aadrick."

This did not seem to satisfy Qidira, but it was going to have to suffice because the small woman turned and moved into the next room. We followed her through the arch into the larger cavern. We passed over the mosaic in the center to the double wooden doors we had seen the night before. As we got closer, I saw the carved design in the doors more clearly: mountains surrounding a lake with a large sun superimposed on the water. Inside of the sun was the image set into the mosaic on the floor: a solid sphere with three smaller orbs around it.

I elbowed Qidira. "There it is again."

Her eyebrows furrowed as we came to a stop.

Tisa knocked, but before anyone inside responded, Qidira gasped. A small brown-skinned dwarf came out of nowhere and clung to her arm with wrinkly hands. The dwarf had a mass of dark hair, wildly framing her oval, age-lined face. She was rounder and shorter than most of the other dwarfs we had seen, and her clothes were a mismatch of what looked like burlap, wool, and a rough green woven fabric that appeared to have been made from plant material. Twigs and leaves adorned her wooly curls. It took me one step to get to Qidira and the odd little woman. I tore her hands off of Qidira's arm, but then Qidira put her hands over mine.

"Elon, it's okay. Don't."

She pushed me behind her. I looked back to the older woman and was instantly enchanted. Her eyes were soft, large, and startlingly blue. They swam like sea water, back and forth, surging and ebbing like waves. They shone like a lantern from beneath thick black lashes, and they seemed as large as the entirety of the rest of her face.

She stammered and finally said in a kind, smooth voice, "I . . . I am sorry, I did not mean to frighten you." She clasped her hands in front of her chest. She smiled at me and her eyes made me feel safe. Reaching out, she touched my arm with both of her hands.

"Hoshi . . . We are kin, you and I." There was a twinkle in her eyes.

My heart thundered. "What did you call me?"

Ignoring my question, she continued, "Oh, so much is being learned . . . so many discoveries . . . so much change. And you"—she turned to Qidira— "anger, yearning . . . and yes, discovery, too."

Qidira's eyebrows shot up in reaction to these assertions about her emotional state.

Tisa made the introductions. "Qidira, Elon, this is Ignacia. She and her daughters are our only remaining ocean sprite descendants and the only dwarfs with mer-blood living here."

That explains the eyes, I thought.

Tisa continued, "She is an empath and a seer, and is one of our healers. She is also the widow of our king's brother."

"Hi," was all I could muster. My mind still reeled with her use of the name I had not heard since my father died.

"It's so nice to meet you," Qidira said.

She took Ignacia's hands in hers and they stared at each other. A faint buzzing filled my head. I knew it was not coming from me and I threw up my mental barriers, attempting to reclaim my mind as my own. I had never been this close to a non-Sidar empath before. I guessed I was picking up her mental static.

Still holding the older lady's hands, Qidira asked Tisa if we would be able to make time to see Ignacia later.

"Of course," Tisa responded. "How long you all stay here is up to you and your journey. We need to introduce you to the rest of the royal family, and then we can address all of the things you want to do."

By this time, the double doors were open and I saw the long room which lay beyond. We said goodbye to Ignacia and followed Tisa into the royal hall.

THE ROYAL FAMILY

*a*s we passed through the arched doorway, we were faced with a long hall lined with polished wooden tables along both sides. We passed down the middle of the flagstone floor and I noticed that the main opening in the ceiling here was in the shape of a sun and scattered around the domed ceiling were other, smaller shapes letting in light. Directly in front of us, at the far end of the room, was a small rise two steps high. On this rise stood another long table and seated behind it were five male and two female dwarfs. One of the females had light colored hair, while the other one had the dark skin of Ignacia.

I saw Aarick sitting two seats away from the center seat, which was more elaborate than the others, with a higher back and green velvet upholstery. Given the majestic nature of the throne, I assumed that the little man settled amidst the carvings was the king, Aadrick. He was an elegantly dressed dwarf with a graying beard and hair that one could tell had originally been black but was now streaked silver with age. Even from this distance, I saw that his dark eyes were keen. They followed everything that happened in the room. As we made our way down the center aisle, the king sat up straight in his chair and folded his hands together on the table in front of him. All chatter in the room ceased.

My strides were short as we closed the distance between the door and the table. As we went, I looked around at the walls. Weavings hung on the stone. They depicted different scenes: battles, love scenes, images from nature. I thought I caught movement out of the corner of my eye, but when I looked directly at the figures, they were still. I diverted my attention to the wall next to one of the love scenes and noticed the couple caress each other before sneaking a chaste kiss. I watched from the corner of my eye, and then looked directly at it. The movement stopped. The male in the image looked like the dwarf king but with less gray. I guessed that this tapestry depicted a love affair with the king and his beloved. The female in the tapestry was not at the table. It was clear, however that her son, Aarick, had inherited her eyes.

As we drew close to the table, chairs were brought out from the wall for us and placed in front of the elevated stage. Tisa left us, climbed the two stairs, and stood at the end of the long, polished table. Aadrick stood up.

"Welcome to both of you. I understand you had a rough time coming through the portal?" He addressed this question to me.

I recalled the slow, searing journey through the rock. "Yes, actually, I did."

"I am sorry about that. I hope you suffered no permanent damages. The magic that makes that port of entry possible also bars against vamphyres. Aarick tells me he worked hard to bring you through, that he was afraid you might not make it." I looked toward Aarick and saw on his face that this was a true statement. Aadrick continued, "But thankfully, you did."

He turned his bright eyes to Qidira and smiled. "And you, our newest fairy visitor. Thank you for coming. I trust the trip through the rock was not as uncomfortable for you?"

"No," Qidira said, returning his smile, "it was quick, I did not feel any discomfort. A little surprise, perhaps, but no pain."

"Tisa has been providing you with everything you need, yes?"

"Yes, thank you," we both said, almost in unison.

"Did you sleep well?"

"Yes, thank you." This time only Qidira answered. I just nodded.

"Good, good." He sat back down and spread his arms out to either side. "Let me introduce you to the current royal council. At the end"—he motioned to the last seat to his right— "is Aarick, whom you have already met. Then my second grandson, Aaldin. Here next to me is my son and the successor to the throne, Aaron." Aaron smiled and nodded.

"On my left"—his arm swept in that direction— "is Aadnon, first son of Aaron. Next to him is Blasi"—he motioned to the darker skinned female two seats away— "daughter of my late brother and his wife. And next to her is Cysta, the granddaughter of one of my cousins." The king folded his hands in front of himself once again. "Now that you know us, let us know more about you."

"I thought you knew who we were, and why we were here." My words sounded more abrasive than I meant them to.

Aadrick smiled and chuckled. "Of course. I do know who you are, Elon. I suppose what I would like is to know more about your intentions." The eyes of everyone at the table were on me.

Frustration rose in my stomach. "Gosh," I said, not trying to hide my sarcasm, "let me see . . . I was sent into the mountains by a vision in my sleep of ancestors who have never contacted me before, asking me for help with something that I had never heard of before. Then, I was painfully and almost fatally sucked through a rock wall, but not before I was almost killed by a river troll. And after I survived the passage into your home, thank you Aarick by the way, I have heard almost nothing but derogatory comments about my ancestry. Honestly, I really haven't had time to sit and ponder my intentions."

Qidira hid a smile.

I continued, with a bit more composure, "All that being said, I suppose you really want to know what I'm planning on doing about the request from the Sidar."

"Yes, actually," Aadrick replied, appearing to ignore my outburst. "So, let us start there. What do you know about the Sidra, the Star?" An unreadable expression adorned his face. Even in its neutrality, however, his continence did not mask the intensity of his unblinking eyes.

"All I know," I said, "is that it came from the planet Sidra, that it somehow has great meaning to the Sidar, and that I was not drawn to Palus by accident." I unconsciously crossed my arms in front of my chest. Then I self-consciously uncrossed them and grasped my hands in my lap.

"Okay, that's a good start."

"Oh, and that something is about to happen to it or because of it . . . presumably having to do with the arrival of the ship in the marshes, and that I am supposed to help in some way that is unique to me."

"Even better." He reclined in his chair and his smile

appeared genuine. "And so, my question becomes"—he sat forward again— "are you planning on doing what needs to be done?"

I rolled my eyes. "Honestly, there's not enough information in that question. You'll have to give me a bit more." Again, my sarcasm was apparent.

Aadrick leaned even further across the table. His eyebrows furrowed and the smile faded from his lips. When he spoke, his voice was low and strong.

"There is a lot at stake here, young one." I bristled and opened my mouth to protest, but he continued without letting me speak. "You know it. I know you do. You are not unintelligent, that I do know about you. You have a lot of the good characteristics that define your various ancestors. You are strong, quick, tough-skinned, empathic, and as far as I can tell, honorable."

I smiled at this last one.

He continued, "You are distinctly capable of carrying out this mission; as you have already pointed out, there is something about you that has caused the Sidar to call for you. So, I ask you again, are you willing to do what needs to be done, *whatever* it is that needs to be done?"

The room was silent. Qidira reached over and put her hand on mine. I looked at her and saw a reassuring smile that said, *Everything is going to be alright.*

I hesitated. Thoughts were developing and evolving in my mind faster than I could process them.

"What does that mean, though?" I chastised myself for the hint of fear I heard in my voice, but I then gave myself a thumbs-up for managing a more respectful tone. "I don't feel right saying yes to something if I don't know what I'm agreeing to. Do you have any idea what 'whatever it takes' might entail?"

His question caused the last couple of days to catch up

with me, again. This time, however, I was in front of a room full of magical beings who might be unfazed if I met with an untimely death. There was no cozy room with dancing light. No space for the vulnerability afforded by alone time with Qidira. Like a firm blow to the chest, I realized I was being asked to think through what starting this journey would mean and to discuss what it might take to end it. Fear of needing an answer without fully grasping the question engulfed me. I wanted to smack him.

I reviewed what I did know: I was going to meet the Sidar. I might even learn more about myself. I knew eventually I would have to fight vamphyres; I was good at that part. But the unknown possibilities past that were overwhelming. I felt my defensiveness melt away and slumped against the back of my chair.

"Honestly, I don't know," I finally continued. "I hadn't thought past the first settlement. Now that I'm here, in a place I never imagined existed, I guess I have to figure out what the next step is going to be."

Aadrick sat back as well and considered me during a long, deep breath. "You are moving on to the next step then?" he finally asked.

"Do I have a choice?"

"We always have a choice."

"No, sometimes we don't."

No one said anything.

Aadrick smiled and rested his elbows on the carved wooden arms of his chair. He placed his fingertips together, creating the appearance of a wise, web-like tower. "Vamphyre or not, your honor shows through. You will always have a place here in Truth, and we will help in whatever way you need in order to carry out your journey." His face was open, and I understood he meant what he said.

"Thank you."

"You are welcome to take a few days, gather information, find some peace, and perhaps create a plan." He must have seen my face because, before I could say anything, he continued, "Yes, we will give you more information in order to come up with a plan, don't worry." His smile was patient. My muscles relaxed once again.

"Here is what we know: the Sidar arrived generations ago, before my grandfather's time as king. They came to the mountains on a moonless night, in a swirl of color from the sky. Some of them fell into the lake, a few landed on the shore. It is sad to say that some of them perished at the hands of the water folk living in the water above us, but we had no way of knowing if they were friend or foe. A few of them quickly found the topside entrance to Truth and were met at the bottom of the main stairwell by our soldiers." He pointed towards the expansive stairway in the main cavern. "They prostrated themselves, desperately requesting help. There were four of them on the floor, and they each spilled something from the front of their robes—the four parts of the Sidra.

"The story goes that once the individual elements were close to each other, they rose into the air and began spinning. If you look at the crest we all wear"—he pointed to his left breast— "you will see the representation we have taken on. A better image can be seen set into the floor of the main cavern. The mosaic was magicked into the stone where the elements originally reunited: a large sphere with a bright light contained in the center, with three smaller spheres orbiting in their individual paths around it." He stared over our heads.

I gazed in surprise at Qidira and whispered, "The sphere thingy."

"I know," she replied through gritted teeth. "Now shhh."

Aadrick continued his story as if we had not spoken. "The center stone began to glow and the peripheral parts whirled so fast they became a blur of color. Soon after the Star was reconstituted, a loud noise reverberated down the stairs from the shores of the lake, and the caves shook. Violent screams issued from up top and Truth was soon invaded by vamphyres. We were unprepared and a lot of our people were lost. The vamphyres found special delight in feeding on any fairy they found, and those they did not drain on that first day, they captured to be eaten later." He snarled and, once again, I was reminded of just how unpopular vamphyres were on Palus.

"When the screams began, the four Sidar stood under the Star in a circle, closed their eyes, and raised their hands. The spinning stopped and the individual parts descended back to their guardians. We ushered them quickly through our tunnel system, but we knew that, without help, they still might be found. We had a high council member who was an almost full-blooded fairy and he created a stone barrier, much like the one you came through yesterday, which led into an unexplored system of caverns.

"Since then we have gained great power from the presence of the Sidra here. Our food is heartier, our animals more bountiful, and our individual ancestral powers are exponentially extended. Our weaving and metallurgy have taken on a new life that was never possible before." He motioned toward the tapestries on the wall. "Yes, they move, and if you have trouble seeing it, it may be because of your vamphyre heritage.

I held back my eye-roll. Instead, I gritted my teeth as he continued.

"We do not see the Sidar much," he continued. "They communicate through Ignacia a great deal, and sometimes they show up in our tunnels. But we know they are there and we feel their protection and care.

"Five days ago, we were visited by a tall female Sidar named Shirah. She warned us about the approaching ship and told us about you. She said you were a Sidar Other who lived among the humans; that you would find us, and that we were to help you not lose your way when you got here. She did not mention you were part vamphyre. I must admit, that came as a surprise. I could not understand why they would call a vamphyre to them. Now, however, I do." He considered me from below a furrowed brow. Then he voiced one of my parents' most treasured beliefs.

"Who you are is not the sum of your parts, Elon, and I should have known better than to make that assumption." His expression swam with the shadow of memories. "Vamphyres have done nothing good for us here. Dwarf blood does not accept vamphirism well. Something about what makes us small, strong, and long-lived interferes with whatever process can 'turn' someone who has been bitten. It does bad things to our people and those that survive the original bite die within a few years." He seemed lost in a memory that I did not want to disturb, so I waited before asking my next question.

"If you don't mind telling me," I eventually said, "what caused them to die? The infected ones, I mean." My parents never told me that the interaction between dwarf genetics and the vamphyre virus was different than with other species. They schooled me extensively on how it interacts with the human genetic material, and how the changes express themselves in successive generations, but I knew nothing of the interaction with dwarfs. Now that I thought about it, it made sense that dwarfs might be of some other lineage, some other beginning, and that their genetic code might be separate from other humanoids.

He breathed deeply and replied with sadness in his voice. "Those that are directly bitten generally become insane. Sometimes they take their own life, and sometimes they are killed by one of their own before they can become violent to those around them. In each case, their skin becomes predictably more sensitive to light and the after-effects of exposure to the sun quickly become malignant. Their skin rots, ulcerates, and is eaten to the bone. If violence does not claim them first, they die from secondary infection or they simply seem to rot from the inside out."

"You said those that are directly bitten, does this mean there are others who are infected in another way? In humans, it can be passed by all bodily fluids, and via genetic code. Perhaps it is the same with dwarfs? Is it passed in another fashion, perhaps via direct inoculation of another or by reproduction?" Curiosity churned my thoughts.

He smiled. "No, they do not bite others. They never grow the teeth most vamphyres have." I self-consciously ran my tongue over my barely pointed canines. "But they sometimes do reproduce." He sighed. "That original raid left some of our people wounded but not dead. There were no vamphyres on this planet prior to their arrival. Those that live in the forest now are defectors who fled the battle. So, we were woefully ignorant to what would happen next. It was a sad time, as we watched the few dozens of our kin who suffered non-fatal attacks heal their physical wounds but change from who they were.

"Before the full change occurred, however, a handful of them created offspring and passed the infliction to their children. One of those who was attacked was married to a royal. She bore a pair of twin daughters before the sickness claimed her. The daughters grew up seemingly unaffected, and one of them married another royal, my great uncle. These daughters lived happy lives but died young of internal sickness. They stopped eating, their skin began to bruise easily, and their breasts deteriorated from the inside. They died painful deaths."

"I've seen this," I interrupted. "It is an uncontrolled growth of tissue in the body. It happens in humans sometimes as well. I've never seen it in pure vamphyres. Do male descendants suffer similar deaths?"

"Yes, however they seem to die bleeding from all parts of their bodies. It is awful, but it limits the amount of vamphyre blood there is in our community, and while it is sad to lose anyone, we see it as a necessary evil to limit the progression."

"This process can occur anywhere in the body, even in the blood," I continued. "If your physiology is similar to the humans at all, then it makes sense that the further you are away from the original infection, the milder the effects would be. Some aspects of the infection show up generations later in a recessive pattern . . ." I found myself falling into scientific mode, but I realized I was being insensitive, that the subject was obviously difficult for Aadrick. I softened my tone. "I'm sorry for your loss. It seems you may have lost someone close to you."

He nodded. "My brother. He died after fighting his wife's father, who was a distant descendant of one of the afflicted. My brother was a pure dwarf; he became infected somehow and died within the month. He left behind one daughter, Blasi." We all turned our eyes toward the dark woman to his left. Tears ran down her proud face and I saw her mother shining out from within her.

Qidira spoke for the first time. "Excuse my ignorance,

I'm not sure I understand all of this fully, but doesn't that make you, dear Blasi, part vamphyre?"

Blasi's sapphire blue eyes flared and her face set in a mask of indignation. "By no means am I a *vamphyre*. My mother was spared, somehow, from . . . the affliction." Her face softened at the mention of Ignacia.

"I'm sorry, I meant no disrespect." Qidira shrunk back in a gesture of apology. Blasi simply nodded.

"Does this mean there are dwarfs who are immune?" I asked, fascinated.

"It appears that those with mer-blood, or any dwarf with water-linked blood, are immune to the effects, yes," Aadrick said.

This information surprised me and made me think again about the interaction of the virus with my own genetic material. Had my mother been infected by my father? She was part river troll, had that spared her? Was it only the mix of dwarf and water-creature genetics that provided protection? The only answer I found in my head was that I was part human and that my genes were passed to me already altered by the vamphyre virus. Bitter sadness stabbed my gut at the thought of my parents.

I pushed my feelings away. To the room I said, "Still, and again, with no disrespect, I would think that the genetic material that makes someone who they are would still contain some of the changes. Blasi, half of who you are came to you from your mother, whose own father was infected. Whether Ignacia was spared or not, she had to hold the code somewhere in her genetic material, which was passed along already altered by the vamphyric condition."

She looked shocked and turned toward the king. "I cannot be . . . I will not be!"

Aadrick reached over and laid a calming hand on top

of hers. Cysta leaned toward her and placed an arm over her shoulders.

To me, Aadrick said, "The Sidar told us you were intelligent." Again, he sighed a deep, strong, sigh, heavy with the weight of the unknown and the burden of duty.

A thought came to mind and I quickly shared it. "Your majesty, I have a strong theory about Other. In my short time here in Truth, I have seen mostly what appear to be those of pure dwarf heritage, although I know there are those with Other blood living here." I glanced at Qidira who nodded with encouragement.

"I believe that when genetic material mixes it creates an entirely new being, a new species, if you will. The vamphyre virus attacks a person's genetic material; it changes it and re-writes it. Whatever that portion coded for before, eye color, tooth shape, skin resiliency and repair, is re-expressed in the host." I was not sure I was making sense, but Aadrick nodded.

"We understand genetics. We track it as well." He turned to the one named Aadnon and said something in a low voice. Aadnon nodded and then, as the king addressed us again, smiled at me. His eyes shone with interest and his smile was warmer than expected. I felt myself blush.

"Before you leave," Aadrick spoke again. "Would you be willing to discuss this further with my grandson, Aadnon? He is a seeker of knowledge and often struggles to find answers to the same questions you are asking."

I glanced at Aadnon's eager face. *How can I say no?*

"Of course, I will." I smiled at Aadnon and I saw the fire of childhood curiosity flare in his dark eyes.

"Good. Now, I apologize: please continue with what you were saying," Aadrick said.

"I'm just saying that Blasi may have vamphyre-altered genes, but that she may be a whole new creature. Her own, new species. Perhaps she is no more vamphyre than Qidira is." Qidira glanced at me with bemused interest at the mention of her name. Then, to the young woman behind the table, I said, "Please don't deny your heritage, Blasi. Whatever has been done to your people in the past is not due to your actions. Because you might carry the blood of one of those you despise does not mean who you are is to be despised, as well." Blasi looked down at me, her face now soft and open, touched by my words. I continued. "All I'm saying is: regardless of what or who we are created by, we are the ones who decide how we move forward in life."

I became self-conscious and felt like I had overstepped a boundary. Who was I to lecture this proud race of people on how to live? I sat back in my chair and looked toward the ground, pulling inwards. "I'm sorry, I didn't mean to be too bold or insulting. I'm sure you think of such things already."

Aadrick chuckled. "My dear, you would have to get up pretty early in the morning to truly be insulting to me. These ones"—he gestured to either side of him— "I am not so sure about. Please do not apologize; it appears we could use a lesson in tolerance." He paused, placing his fingertips together once more. "While we fancy ourselves as accepting of those who are looking for peace, justice, and balance, I now see how hateful we have been toward anything vamphyre. I guess we all have our prejudice."

"Generations of hate is hard to extinguish, whoever we are," I responded.

Aadrick considered me, gently biting his lower lip. He nodded. "True."

There was an expectant pause and then the king pulled out of his contemplative reverie. "Let us return to talk of your journey. As I said, we are hoping you will take a few days to figure out what you feel you need to do next. We will provide you with food and clothing for the journey, and we will, of course, return your weapons. We will also provide you with new ones, if you wish."

If we wish? Who would turn down dwarf weaponry? What I had was good, Qidira had made it, but I could only imagine what was available here.

I attempted to keep the child-like glee from my voice as I responded, "Thank you, I would like that." I resituated my composure to better reflect how, at least in my estimation, someone saddled with this much responsibility should appear. I cleared my throat before moving on to my next question. "When it is time for us to go to the Sidar, will you be able to take us to them?"

The king shifted and appeared uncomfortable. "Well, we were hoping you might have that information. We can take you in the general direction of their caves, but we do not know how to get through the rock. The fairy that sent them through all those years ago also sealed it to our magic. Obviously, the Sidar can get through, so perhaps you have information of which you are unaware that will help you when the right time comes?"

I gaped, my mouth open. My powers were growing, for sure, but I thought this was going a little too far. I had just been dragged, almost fatally, through a solid rock wall. And now he thought I might be able to magic my way through another one?

Aadrick continued, "In the meanwhile, are you hungry? I, myself, am ready for lunch. Anyone else?"

Heads bobbed along the length of the table.

"Wait." Qidira's loud voice cut through the low chatter that sprung up among the council. Aadrick looked back toward us with surprise. "Where is my son? Where is Tariq?" She was perched on the edge of her seat, ready to launch at any dwarf who dared rob her of the answer she desperately desired.

Aadrick settled back into his chair, and said, "Ah, of course, Tariq . . . He is here, somewhere. Dear Qidira . . . perhaps, well, perhaps I should defer your question to Ignacia, would that be alright with you? I promise Tisa will take you right to her."

Qidira looked toward Tisa, who appeared ready to do whatever the king requested of her.

Qidira pursed her lips and her nostrils flared before she answered, "Sure."

I stood and, with a glance back at her, I approached the table to shake the king's hand. His skin was warm and his grasp firm. He looked me straight in the eyes and said, "We will meet again soon, Elon."

I smiled before turning to follow Tisa and Qidira out of the room.

THE LAKE

isa did not, in fact, lead us directly to Ignacia. First, she took us back to the table where we had eaten breakfast and brought us more food. When we were done, she returned to us, handed us soft wool sweaters, and led us to the bottom of the wide steps at the west end of the main cavern. Looking up, all I saw were white stairs disappearing into darkness.

"Does this lead to the outside?" I asked.

"It does," Tisa said, "but right now there are only a few who are allowed to go topside. Since the arrival of the ship in the marshes, we have sealed most of our ports of entry. We will go up, but there is a point when I will have to leave you with directions for the remainder of the trip to Ignacia's."

"Ignacia lives outside?" Qidira asked.

"Her home is both up top and within the caves. She prefers to be at the waterside, and so she spends a great deal of her time up there. She has asked that we direct you to her front door, on the shores of the lake."

Qidira and I exchanged a glance and, with a quick shrug, I began climbing the stairs.

We ascended steadily through rising darkness. Spaced evenly along the wall, torches hung in metal bases. The flames flickered, casting shadows across the marble stairs. Finally, we came to a small landing that had a wooden door.

We stopped and Tisa addressed us. "Go through here. Follow the tunnel and do not take any of the turns. When you emerge into the cavern at the end of the tunnel you will see light past the small waterfall. You will have to climb the rocks down to the stream bed and follow the water out to the lake. Once there, continue to the right. You will pass what looks like a massive rock slide. That is what is covering the entrance to this stairway. Pass the rock slide and hidden in a crag in the mountainside you will find a small archway covered in rough, heavy fabric. This is Ignacia's place. She will be expecting you. Do you have any questions?" She handed me one of the torches from the wall.

We both shook our heads and soon Qidira opened the door. We immediately felt a blast of cold air. Our torch wavered and we stepped into the cold dampness of a narrow tunnel. We closed the door behind us and donned the sweaters Tisa had given us.

The tunnel was small and I had to walk bent over; Qidira's head just barely cleared the rough ceiling. We both had to dodge the occasional root tips that struggled down through the rock. We followed the tunnel upwards, turning in what felt like a rising spiral. As we climbed, the air became steadily cooler. We encountered smaller openings in the side of the tunnel that I would not have fit through, and once there was a portion of the floor that had almost completely fallen away. We heard the echo of dripping water, but it was too dark for us to see down into the sink-hole. I stepped over the opening in the floor and reached back to help Qidira jump across.

The air grew even colder, and I was starting to wish for the pajamas from the night before, when the tunnel narrowed even more. I felt like I was going to either scream out of claustrophobia or laugh hysterically for no reason, or both. Thanks to the Gods, we soon reached a steep opening into a high, narrow crack of a cave.

I looked up but could see neither light nor the roof of the crevice we were now facing. There was just enough room on the fissure's floor for a small chaotic path of water to run between the uneven rock. We climbed down from our crack in the wall onto the slippery surface below. It took us a while to make our way along the gently downward sloping stream bed. As we went, the walls widened, illuminated by the flickering torch I still carried. After a few moments, we heard the sound of water falling, and soon we saw a small glimmer of light ahead of us.

The waterfall we came to was really just a trickle, but the height of the cavern magnified the noise of the ten-click drop. I looked over the edge and was not happy to see a dark, jagged floor below us.

"Do you see any stairs over there?" I asked Qidira, who had ventured the small distance to the other wall of the cavern.

"No."

I inspected the cliff edge to my left and saw no way down.

"'*Climb the rocks*'—psh," I said to myself.

Qidira joined me as I stared at the wide, shallow crack in the rock face a few clicks past the base of the falls. It glared at us like a wicked, twisted smile, its broken teeth sticking into the mouth at different angles. I looked back toward the ground directly below us.

"Do you think you could hover down?" she asked. "I know it takes a lot, but perhaps you will have more strength with the Sidar close by."

I thought about it and really did not feel like testing the idea with the inhospitable ground we were facing. I decided to try and levitate over the water where we were first.

I had never concentrated on flying before; I had always just done it. I thought about wanting to move away from the ground and all of a sudden it was as though something pushed me upwards. My father had explained the mechanism of flying when I was young: vamphyres have a physical energy that they place between themselves and whatever they are flying over. The energy has to be constantly adjusted if one is flying over uneven ground, and this was the part that always wore me out the most. Now, hovering higher over the rock than I wanted to, I felt something physical between me and the ground. I moved toward the edge and tentatively flew out over the drop-off.

It was not long before I regretted it. The floor disappeared beneath me and I plummeted quickly. In a panic, I dropped the torch. I heard it hit the water below and extinguish with a hiss. I threw what energy I could out through the bottom of my feet, reaching for the ground with my mind. I did not stop falling, but the effort was enough to slow me. I landed with a rough bump on the boulders and slipped, falling hard on to my backside.

"Ouch," I exclaimed, more out of frustration than pain.

Qidira's voice echoed down from above me, "Are you okay?"

"Yeah, nothing really hurt but my pride."

"And we all know that could use the occasional bruise."

"Funny. You should talk, *fairy*." I got up and wiped at the wet seat of my pants. I could just make out the outline of Qidira's little head leaning over the edge of the cliff, and I heard her chuckle.

"What now?" she asked.

I looked around. From this viewpoint I still could not see a safe way to get her down. "Would you be willing to try riding with me?" I sounded more assured than I felt.

"Do you really think you can do it?"

"Sure." I replied, not hiding the sarcastic doubt in my voice. I closed my eyes and focused energy through my feet again. This time I also threw out my hands, opening them wide. I tried to imagine pushing myself off of the ground with both my hands and my feet, and when I opened my eyes to gauge my progress, I was hovering well above Qidira.

"Oops," I said, descending back to her.

"How do you feel?"

"Fine." I noticed that my energy level did not appear to have been affected. "Better than I normally do after flying. Get onto my back."

I instructed her to latch her ankles together around me and when I felt like she was secure I rose off of the ground again. I did not go as far with the extra weight, but I felt more in control than I had when I tried it the first time. Concentrating hard, I took us over the edge. Again, I felt the ground slip out from under me, but this time the energetic footing was slippery and chaotic. I realized I had gone out over the stream and what I was feeling was the moving surface of the water instead of solid rock. We landed with a cold splash into the stream below.

"Nice," Qidira said from my back. "It was sketchy

there for a moment, but I knew that if we fell you would break my fall, so I wasn't too worried."

I laughed. "Qidira, I would never let you fall, you know that."

"Yes, I do." She squeezed my shoulders.

I kept her on my back as we moved down the stream bed and her weight made me more conscious of where I stepped. My boots kept the cold out for a while, but as I continued along the stream, the biting water leaked through the seams and stung my feet. Qidira shivered against my back.

I carefully picked across what was left of the cavern to the narrow mouth through which the water flowed. The opening was close to the ground, short and wide. I let Qidira down and she found a space on the right side of the gap just large enough for her to pull herself through on her belly.

I stood in front of the place where she had just left and knew that I would not be able to make it out that way. The only area wide enough for me was where the water happily babbled its way to the lake. Cold bit the pit of my stomach as I thought about having to get wet in order to get out.

I lowered myself onto my stomach, dipping into the running water. I did not feel the cold at first, but after a few short moments of pulling myself along, my fingertips started to feel numb. My skin burned in response to the icy mountain run-off.

By the time I reached the other side, I was panting in response to the cold. I stood up and instantly my clothes froze against me. I was grateful for my thick skin, but even that could not keep this kind of cold out. I jumped out of the stream to join Qidira on the edge of the clear mountain lake.

The view around us was breathtaking. The water in front of us was clear and calm, smooth and quiet, no doubt brought down from the frigid peaks via tributaries like the one I had just dunked myself in. I saw details of the bottom far out into the lake. I walked closer to the edge and looked out as far as I could, trying to see if the windows into Truth were visible. It must have been very deep because, in spite of the clarity of the water, the ground disappeared from view and I could not see anything.

It appeared there were mountains on all sides of the water. The shores were lined with pine trees, with occasional fingers of vegetation extending out into the glassy calm. Ice clung to this ground. In some areas, the mountains rose more gradually and there, trees grew up the side of the hills. As I looked around, I searched for a way out of this bowl in the mountain tops, but I did not find one. No valley, no path, no wide fissure. There was no exit apparent from where we stood.

"I don't like feeling trapped," I said aloud.

"What?" Qidira replied. "I can't hear you through the ice that has formed over my ears." She was walking in place. She pulled her hands into the arms of her sweater and moved them from her ears to her nose and then back in an effort to warm herself.

"Okay, let's go." I made exaggerated movements with my hands, signing that we should start moving again. She released a hearty laugh and the resulting echo startled us both. Across the lake, a flock of birds rose from the trees and we froze, looking around and listening for any other sound. We exchanged a glance and then wordlessly hurried toward the large rockslide to our right.

Tisa was right. It looked like the mountain had broken apart and fallen down into the lake. If there had been any kind of majestic door there before, there was no sign of it now.

Qidira and I climbed the rocks quickly and carefully. She pulled her hands out of the sleeves of her shirt in order to have a better grip on the stone and I saw that her skin was red and angry. When we reached the other side, we saw a crack in the stone that looked like someone had tried to cut a wedge out of the mountainside, not too big, but smooth and straight up.

"You think?" I said.

"Let's see," Qidira replied.

As we approached the crevice the air grew warmer. When we entered the shadow of the rock, I did not miss the pale sunlight or the cold wind. The rock seemed warmer on both sides and it radiated out to meet us. As the crack narrowed, we saw a small archway covered with roughhewn cloth, which gathered on the ground.

"Should we knock?" I asked.

"Do you think it would work?" Qidira said, sarcastically.

I rolled my eyes. "I don't know. Should we just walk in?"

Almost as in response to our conversation, a voice floated through the fabric, "Yes, yes, come on in."

Qidira flashed me a look of superiority.

"What was that for?" I asked with a chuckle.

She did not answer; she just pushed the fabric to one side and passed through the doorway. A rush of warm air hit my face and I hurried to follow her.

THE STAR BASIN

I had to bend over in order to enter the small room, and when I straightened up, I saw an inviting fire burning on the opposite wall from the door. A sweet herbal smell emanated from the flames. Ignacia was seated at a wooden easel next to the fire. She scratched furiously at the parchment in front of her and held up one hand as we entered. Without looking up she motioned to a pile of pillows and low wooden stools which stood against the wall to our right.

She continued to work at the document, brow furrowed, for another hundred breaths. While she worked, I inspected the room from where we sat. Herbs hung from the ceiling, and across from us was a set of shelves, one of which was full of jars and baskets. Next to the shelves was a stone basin. It appeared to have been one big rough boulder, out of which a center bowl had been carved. I got up to look inside, but Ignacia again put up her hand, indicating for me to stop. She then waved it to tell me to sit back down. I did as she directed.

I looked more closely at the fireplace and noticed that on the right side of the hearth a small doorway was cut into the stone. The opening housed a small wooden door, which was shut. I was tempted to go and open it but had a feeling I would be admonished again, so I chose to stay seated.

Qidira nudged me and pointed to the shelves. I followed her finger and saw a glass flask of swirling blue-green liquid. It took a breath or two before I saw what had caught her attention: every now and then a small face passed by as the water moved around. We stared, trans-fixed, until Ignacia stepped into our line of sight. We both looked up, startled.

"Are my pixies interesting to you?" She retrieved the flask.

Pulling over a low, well-worn stool, Ignacia sat in front of us. She held the glass up in front of our eyes. Now we had a better view of the faces swimming in the liquid: they were smiling and laughing, and, occasionally, we would see two holding on to each other in what looked like a friendly tussle.

The pixies were of various colors. Their skin appeared leathery and there was webbing between their fingers and their toes. "They sometimes nest in the lake, but this batch found their way into the river down below. The swirling keeps them happy and makes them feel like they are living in running water." She held up the flask and we saw the backs of creatures lying down on the bottom and the tiny feet of what must have been juveniles hopping or dancing around.

"When I need their help, I stop the motion and they all come to the top." She waved her hand around the container. The swirling slowed and soon stopped altogether. In a few moments, a rainbow of tiny little heads popped up from beneath the water. They all looked questioningly at Ignacia and I heard a series of high-pitched melodies. The noise seemed to mean something to her and she answered normally.

"Thank you, no, I am fine. I just wanted to show our visitors who you were." They all swam to the glass wall and waved at us. We tentatively waved back.

"Now," she said, getting up and replacing the pixies back on their shelf, "how are you two?" She sat down, again, with her hands in her lap. She watched us intently with her now clear blue eyes.

Qidira and I looked at each other, and I said, "Well, I'm cold as crap, and I am feeling overwhelmed, excited, and a little scared. How about you, Qid?"

"I second the cold, and am, myself, anxious to find my son."

Ignacia smiled, "I am happy you are here, happy that you found your way. Let me get you new clothes." She disappeared past a tapestry hanging on the wall next to the shelves, returning almost immediately with a stack of clothing made from the same material as the pajamas we slept in the night before.

"Sweet," I said.

"Indeed," Qidira added.

We quickly changed. Ignacia took our wet clothes and hung them on hooks over the fire. I heard hissing as the dripping water hit the hearth.

"Now, dear Qidira," Ignacia began.

Qidira appeared ready to receive information

"Tea?" Ignacia asked.

Qidira's eyes flared. I put a hand on her knee. Ignacia handed us each a large, steaming, earthen flask. We thanked her, and I eagerly wrapped my hands around the warmth. The tea itself was sweet, like the smell that emanated from the fire. I took a careful sip and felt the warmth spread down my throat and through my stomach.

"Thank you," I said.

Qidira sipped the liquid, watching the older lady over the edge of the mug.

"Good, good. Now." Ignacia closed her eyes, folded her hands in her lap, and drew in a deep breath through her nose. She let out a low sound with her exhale and I felt a warm wind winding around my body like a cocoon. My stomach quivered.

"Right," Ignacia said, opening her eyes. She looked toward me. "You, Elon, are fighting me. Are you aware of this?"

"No," I replied. I reflected inwards, trying to see if I felt I was fighting something. "I guess I feel apprehensive, but . . . I wasn't *consciously* fighting anything."

"No," Qidira interjected, "it's just your baseline belligerence." I elbowed her.

"No . . . hmmm . . ." Ignacia continued, "I am just trying to settle things in here and it seems that you are unsettled. I expected to be able to read your feelings more easily given your genetics . . . but you are blocking me. That's okay, trust is earned; it's natural for you to be wary of me." She paused. "Let us start in a different manner then. How about I attempt to answer your questions and let you get to know me."

"Okay, sounds good." I had not thought I was being difficult at all, so whatever she wanted to do was fine by me.

"I will go first," Qidira interrupted as Ignacia began to talk. "Where is Tariq?"

Ignacia's smile was kind. "Of course, my dear, I will get to that. All in good time."

Qidira sat back with her arms crossed, not at all satisfied with the response.

Ignacia continued speaking to me. "I believe your first question is about kinship."

Her statement annoyed me. "Sure. You said we were kin. I don't see any Sidar in you, and even though I know your father had the virus, I don't think you have any vamphyre either. I definitely don't see any troll . . ." I chuckled. "Are you part human? Because I'm not dwarf, and I know I don't have any sprite or mer-folk in me."

"Are you sure about that?" She leaned forward, smiling.

"I . . . I'm pretty sure, yeah."

"Where do you think you got your eyes from? Are those vamphyre eyes? They are not from the Sidar, or the troll, for that matter."

"I got my mother's eyes. She was half human."

"Well, I don't know for sure from where they came, your father or your mother, but I can tell you, from one sprite to the next, you are part ocean sprite."

My eyebrows shot up and I stared at her, my face blank. "Are you joking?" I looked from her to Qidira. I looked back to Ignacia. "You're not joking. I'm not, I know I'm not."

"Why do you protest so much? Is this a bad thing? Is it so wrong that you have something else in your heritage of which you were unaware?" She settled back. "Or is it that you cling so tightly to the knowledge of who you are that this new idea throws you off?"

Qidira looked at me with the annoying half-smile she uses when she thinks she is right and is waiting for me to see it.

"What, Qidira? Like you knew anything about this."

"Don't yell at me," she said with a laugh, her smile widening. "She's right is all. Elon, please, you know as well as I do that you cling to your heritage as if you were clinging to the physical form of your parents. If this is true, then all it offers is more information about, I'm guessing, your mother. And really, you gave that whole speech to Blasi earlier, so take your own advice for once." Then, under her breath, she added, "Even though I know it's against your stubborn nature."

I glared at her. Taking a deep breath, I sat back against the warm stone wall. The realization that Qidira was right crept over me, but I waited a few extra moments before letting her know. I was not in the mood for her insufferable righteousness.

"Alright," I admitted. My exasperation was almost palpable. "Fine, you're right. And don't laugh at me or I will poke you right in your little fairy eye."

She made a kissing gesture in my direction.

Ignacia interrupted our spat. "If you don't believe me, would you like to see?"

We both swung our heads toward her.

"What?" Qidira asked. I just looked at the older woman, my face blank.

"Come over to the stone." Ignacia rose and moved to the basin next to the shelves.

As I approached, I saw that the inside was completely smooth and appeared to be a perfect half-circle filled with clear water. The stone on the inside of the boulder was different than that of the outside. Whereas the outside was rough and cream-colored, the inside was dark blue-gray, with flecks of material imbedded among its swirls that glinted in the firelight. Something caught my eye. I could not see exactly what it was, but every now and then the light danced and something shone out at me.

"This is a star basin," Ignacia said. "It was a gift from the Sidar. We call it the basin of truth." She put a finger in and swirled it in a large circle. The water became cloudy and amorphous images swam across the surface until the water settled again.

"What does it do?" I asked.

"Why don't you try it and tell us," Ignacia said.

I looked sideways at her. "The last time I trusted an unknown magic stone object I was almost killed by a river troll."

"And you made it into Truth, did you not?" Ignacia's smile did not falter.

I did not answer but stared into her shifting eyes. With a tip of her head towards the stone, she stepped aside and motioned for me to approach the basin. Soon I stood with my hips leaning against the stone.

"The first thing I need you to agree to is to follow directions. Can you do that?"

Her patronizing question, asked innocently enough, grated at my already raw emotions. Qidira's chuckle from her resting spot on the pillow did not help.

"Shush, you," I spat over my shoulder. "I'm not that bad."

Qidira snorted. "Sure, okay. Just pay attention, my belligerent bestie."

I held back an eye-roll and returned my attention to Ignacia. "Okay. I will follow directions."

Her smile remained calm. "Put your finger, or hand, into the water and swirl to the right, in a circle. Not to the left, do you understand?"

I nodded.

"Know that the more of you that is submerged in the basin, the stronger the vision will become."

I shrugged, unsure of what she was trying to tell me. "Okay."

"Ready?" she asked. After my affirming nod she indicated for me to start the process. I dipped my hand into the water and began the circular movement. "Good, like that. Keep the circles going until the images begin to form."

I moved two fingers through the water and colors swam on the cloudy surface. I removed my hand and as a drop of water left my fingers and hit the swirling water, echoes of waves moved outward. Soon, the water became smooth and I saw an image I did not understand.

I felt Qidira move to my side, her chest even with the side of the basin. "What is that?"

"I . . . I don't know." A light flickered, like fire, and then a bird of prey flew through the flames.

"Sidar, vamphyre." Ignacia's voice drew our attention to her. "It is showing you the powers you possess. Keep watching."

We turned back to the water in time to see the flames recede. As a wave crashed against a shore, the last of the fire was extinguished. Instead of sand, however, it looked like the water was hitting solid stone. The shore rotated until it was vertical. Gradually, the wall gave way and the wave poured over an edge into a green field of flowers and grass.

The image changed again and the flowers and grass changed into fish, turtles, and sea creatures. Soon, the animals smiled at me. They gathered into a mob and swam quickly toward the top of the basin. I jumped back, expecting them to burst through the surface and fly out into the room. They did not, however, and I felt silly.

"Come back, it's okay," Qidira assured me.

When I got back to the basin everything was settled. The water was clear except for a bright light shining at the bottom. I squinted, trying to make out the shape. It was round, but there was something else... warmth and acceptance radiated toward me... three orbs split from the center and drifted away. I could not have looked away if I wanted to. Soon, a figure swam among the wandering satellites.

Strom.

I plunged my hand into the basin, but he disappeared. I moved my arm around, trying to find him.

Ignacia yelled, "Elon, don't!"

But it was too late. The water turned dark and, with much difficulty, I withdrew my arm. Ignacia darted between me and the stone, one hand on the side of the basin and one hand on my chest. "You may not want to see this. You moved your whole arm in a full circle in the opposite direction than before. Your fears are manifesting themselves in the water instead of your strengths. Most people think they know their fears, but the power with which you conjured them might be too much." Her eyes swam and I felt the warm cocooning feeling. I let it happen this time, consciously pulling it around me.

"I've come this far." My voice was small.

"Okay . . ." Ignacia eventually conceded, dropping her hand from my chest. "I will help you as much as I can."

I moved back against the stone, settling in next to her. At first, I did not understand what I was seeing. The image was an undulating mass of lines and dots. Soon, however, the individual components cleared, the lines became legs and the dots eyes. A swarm of insects devoured what was left of dead flesh and soon bone was visible. The view panned out and I saw the remnants of a rotting bird laying on dry sand. The image became still larger and showed a desert, with hot sun punishing the carrion on the ground.

The image continued to grow, and, as it moved further away, I saw nothing but orange-yellow sand. Nothing. On the whole planet. We lost sight of the dead bird and were soon among the stars. We passed planet after planet of nothing, nothing but hot, unrelenting sun. An eternal day with no night.

My heart raced and I reached out for the psychic cocoon Ignacia was holding around me.

At my side she whispered, "I am here, but your fear is inside. That is a place I cannot touch."

Qidira's hand covered mine, but I pulled away, afraid I was going to somehow hurt her. I stared at the water as I zoomed past planet after planet of desolation. I could not stop it. I reached my hands toward the water to try and put an end to the vision, but Ignacia held me firmly.

"Let it play out, Elon. Close your eyes if you must, but let it finish," she said.

I did not close my eyes and, soon enough, the image changed. My heart sunk; my gut burned. My parents were at the bottom of the basin, lying on even more hot sand. Their flesh was completely desiccated. Their dermis was drawn taut against their bones, every rib discernable through their scorched and shriveled skin. They looked at me and their dry lids scraped across familiar eyes. Tears streamed down my face and my hands started to tremble.

At first, my mother's mouth moved but I did not hear any words. As she extended a hand toward me, her words formed in my mind. *"Go away. You are not ours. We do not love you. We do not know you."*

Then my father spoke, and I heard him in my mind. *"You left us. We waited here for you, but you forgot about us. Hoshi, you are dead to me."*

I half-heartedly strained against Ignacia's strong arms, and I felt Qidira grab me around my waist as my knees gave out. What came next, however, made her let go.

Qidira's face swam in the water. Again, the image grew clearer as we pulled away and I saw the rest of her: head separated violently from her body, arms and legs strewn across a rocky crevice. Her heart was ripped from her chest and blood dripped from the stones.

As the scene grew, Strom's empty eye sockets filled the basin. His corpse danced an eerie jig, his legs and arms separated from his body. When he spoke, the words came from a gash in his neck, the same gash that had triggered such heartache for me back in the town square. His words escaped amidst oozing blood, "*I trusted you to keep me safe and you failed.*" Air bubbled from the exposed structures of his throat and his individual parts fell away, shattering against the rocks near Qidira.

The picture continued to zoom out and I saw every being on Palus dead. Bodies, dismembered and decaying, lay strewn across barren mountains. Qidira's mouth alone swam to the surface. The teeth, covered in blood, shone from her glowing smile. Soon, her lips moved, and again I heard her voice in my mind. "*You were too late. You're always too late. When I need you, you're never there.*"

Anger, fear, and feral need rose through my whole body and burst from my throat before I realized what was happening. "*No!*"

I broke free of Ignacia and thrust myself into the water, grabbing at it with both arms. There was nothing there, nothing but me splashing water over the sides of the basin, onto the earthen floor. I collapsed onto the ground. Covering my face with my hands, I rocked back and forth, sobbing. I could not erase the image of my parents, Strom, or Qidira from my mind. I rubbed my eyes, trying to scrub away the anguish, but the images refused to be purged.

A guttural noise escaped my lips as I bolted to my feet and faced the two women in front of me. I did not know what to do. I stood there, panting, hands clenched, with tears flowing down my face.

"Make it go away," I begged. "I keep seeing them . . . Please, make it go away." I dropped to my knees, grabbed the front of Ignacia's clothes, and wept into her shoulder. She placed her arms around me and held me until I was finished.

When I finally pulled away, I wiped my eyes of the last few tears and turned to Qidira. I hugged her with all my strength.

"Did you see it, too?" I asked. She nodded. "Could you hear what you said or was that just for me?"

Tears glistened in her eyes. "Just you."

I hugged her again, pulling her into me as if we could meld into one and I would never have to worry about her again.

She sputtered and gasped as she tried to speak, "I know that was hard, but really, please let me go, I can't breathe. Remember your strength, my friend." I released my grip and she dropped to the floor. She caught her breath and then wrapped her arms around my waist once more.

"Don't worry Elon, it's okay. Everything is going to be alright," she cooed.

"It's not okay, Qidira." I pulled her to arm's length. "Did you see? Didn't you see?"

"I know, I did . . ."

Ignacia interrupted, "Elon, do not dwell in your fears. If you focus on your fears, your fears increase. If you focus on your strength, your strength will increase. Come, sit down."

She motioned to the seat by the fire, but I chose the pillows upon which we had been sitting before. Qidira picked up a nearby blanket and spread it across my shoulders. She rubbed my back and I focused on my breathing.

We sat in silence. Ignacia handed me a fresh mug of steaming, sweet tea and it calmed me. She and Qidira chatted superficially about what had happened since we arrived in Truth, and when I was feeling less shaken, I joined the conversation.

"Ignacia, do you know what the shining thing at the bottom was?"

"I thought that would be obvious."

Had I not been so emotional I might have managed an eye-roll. As it was, I simply stared at her.

"It was the Sidra, my dear."

"The Star thing, really?" Hot tea stung my throat as I swallowed a mouthful quicker than intended.

"Yes, really."

"Why was Strom there?" I looked from Ignacia to Qidira and back again.

"The young man?" Ignacia asked.

Qidira answered for me. "He was our friend, he . . ." Her voice trailed away and she rested her forehead against my shoulder.

"He was taken from you. I saw that. Attacked in the marsh, correct?"

Qidira and I exchanged glances and Ignacia smiled. "We empaths often see more than we expect. For example, I am sure that when you woke up this morning you did not expect to be confronted by your primal sense of duty and its corresponding fear of failure."

I frowned. On any other day I might have argued with her about what the images meant. Given what I just felt, however, I knew that nothing would explain the images better than her assertions. My frown deepened as I attempted to internalize this truth.

Ignacia graciously shifted the conversation back to the images in the star basin. "What else do you remember?"

I cleared my throat and sifted through my recent memories. "I thought the fire was a representation of my Sidar powers, but I guess it was part of the Sidra, the Star, right?" She nodded. "And I got the bird thing, vamphyre, like you said. Then the water and stone, I assumed they were the troll part. The rest I could guess at, but . . ."

"Well, you saw the sea. That was your power as an ocean sprite."

"Huh . . ." I said, to no one in particular. I looked at the ground, remembering the images in the bowl. "And the creatures that came toward me? I don't understand what that meant." I sipped my tea.

"Sprites are the protectors, the magical manifestations of their origins. Part of who you are is the physical manifestation of the ocean. Sprites hold differing powers, and yours is over the creatures of the sea. They come to you, they respond to you. Have you ever had that experience?"

"No," I said, "I don't think so." I loved the ocean, but I had no specific memories that matched this description.

"Well"—Ignacia sighed— "it is in there, it is in you. It is in your eyes. As for the Sidra, I thought for sure that part would ring clear in your heart."

As I was returning to myself, my annoyance flared bright and new. "Call me dumb then because it didn't. I get that I am Sidar and that the Sidra holds powers for us, is that the obvious part?" My voice was biting, but she seemed to ignore this.

"The Sidra is what you are here for, and I do not just mean in this mountain at this time. It is what you are on this planet for. It has *everything* to do with your powers, everything to do with who you are. The Sidar in you is pure and un-diluted: you are a quarter pure Sidar. That is part of your strength right now. You would do well to remember that." She said the last part with unmistakable reproof. I guess she had not ignored my surliness after all.

Qidira jumped in, "Speaking of the Sidar, would you know how to find them? Aadrick was cryptic about their location in these mountains. Do you think you would be able to help us?"

"I can, and I will. But Qidira, my dear, let us return to the real question that is weighing heavy on your heart."

Even though this was the moment she had waited for, Qidira's eyes showed fear and sadness as she asked, "Do you know where Tariq is?"

"No, I do not." Ignacia leaned forward and put a hand on Qidira's knee. "What I do know is that Tariq is in the mountains. He is one of the Untraceables."

"What . . . what does that mean?" Qidira sputtered, wiping at the tears spilling down her cheek.

"There is a section of the dwarf population with Sidar in them who have fled into the caves. They leave no trace of themselves, and they block all attempts at psychic connection. Tariq joined them a couple of years ago. We were sorry to see him go; he was our last fairy."

"What do these Untraceables do? Why did they leave?" I asked.

"There is a story about the Sidra. In the beginning, when the Sidar first arrived and settled into the caves, they scattered the four different parts of the Star across the planet. The Untraceables believe that if they can find all of the parts and reunite them . . . well, it gets a little unclear from there. Some say they want power and glory, others say they want to once and for all defeat the vamphyres. No one can say except the nomads themselves."

"Have you tried looking for them?" I asked.

"I, myself, have not, however, a few have tried, although half-heartedly, to be honest. The ones who leave are Other who never felt they fit in, and by believing this they created a self-fulfilling prophecy. They rarely left behind any family. Actually, there is only one family member who has been left with us." She looked at Qidira, who looked at me with annoyance in her shifting eyes. I backed away from the rising heat, letting Qidira know that I saw what was brewing.

She rolled her eyes and looked back to Ignacia. "Yes, and . . .?" She asked impatiently. She was sitting on the edge of her chair like she was ready to pounce at any moment.

"Tisa."

"Tisa? Tisa . . . what?" I said, confused.

"Really, Elon? Tisa was the one who was left behind." Qidira rolled her eyes again before turning back to Ignacia. "Sorry, go on."

"Tisa is the daughter of one of the Untraceables. She was left behind after her mother died. She has been raised by the royals. Her mother died of long-passed-down vamphirism. I think the royals wanted to watch Tisa for signs of the same."

Ignacia got up and dragged a rocking chair over to where we were. She sat down and began rocking—back and forth, back and forth—the rockers scratching on the freshly swept earth floor. It was a calming sound yet mournful in its cadence. She stared at the wall. Qidira, still sitting on the edge of her seat, held out her hands, palms up, toward me in a gesture of annoyed impatience. I tried to give her a calming look, telling her to relax. She just crossed her legs and threw her arms across her top knee.

There were a few moments of silence, but then Ignacia said, "Tisa had a beloved. They were wedded for less than a season when he left, too." She continued to rock. "I believe he did so to find her father." She continued to stare at the wall above our heads.

"Are you saying," I said slowly, comprehension dawning, "that Tariq is Tisa's beloved?"

Ignacia nodded and without moving her head she looked down at Qidira.

"Are you saying that my child got married"—Qidira stood up abruptly— "and didn't tell me?"

"Qidira, really, the least of our problems now is Tariq's eloping. Really. Sit down." I put a hand on her arm and tried to pull her down. She resisted but eventually gave in, settling closer to me this time.

"Did . . . do they have any children?" she asked.

"No, no children," Ignacia answered.

We all sat in silence.

It was Qidira who spoke first. "So, he left her to look for her father . . ." The beginnings of pride and hope showed on her face.

"That is what I believe. Some think he left because he is Sidar. Others actually thought he returned to you." She closed her eyes. "Qidira, your son is nearer than you think. Elon, it will be up to you to call to him."

"What? Me?" I stammered.

"Yes dear, you are the Sidar here, and you are the one with the power through the rocks . . . or did you miss that part of your basin vision?"

"Uh . . . I guess I did. Power over rocks?"

"I said through rocks," Ignacia corrected.

"Whatever." I would sort out the semantics of my

evolving powers later. My mind clung to the idea that I might be able to locate Qidira's son. "What does this calling to him entail?"

"Well, you are Sidar, you can call to him."

Not very helpful, I thought. "They always come to me; I've never reached out to them."

Qidira turned fully to face Ignacia. "Could she do it? Can you teach her how? Oh Elon, would you try, please?" Her expectant eyes were bright and she clung to my hand with both of hers.

"Of course, I'll try honey, you know that." I placed my free hand over Qidira's.

"Elon, I cannot tell you how the power works," Ignacia said, "but it has something to do with the strength of the troll, the power of the vamphyre, and, of course, the empathy of the Sidar."

I remembered what happened in the marsh with the vamphyre ship. "Once . . . I was able to 'see' through a solid object. I felt people on the other side, but I could not tell where they were. I've only done it once, though."

"Wonderful," Ignacia said. "Then you at least know what it feels like."

"I guess . . . But I'm seeing a potential problem . . . if I can figure out how to tap into this power of connection with the Sidar, how do I weed through all of the Sidar in the mountains? I know there are the pure ones . . ." The thought that this might lead me to the sect who called me here entered my mind. I might not only be able to locate Tariq for Qidira, but I might also solve at least one mystery of this journey.

The idea of finding the Sidar caused excitement to form in my gut, but along with it came fear. The sooner I found the Sidar and learned or did what I was brought here to do, the sooner I would have to return to the marsh and fight the vamphyres. Actually, if I was honest with myself, I was excited about fighting them, especially after hearing the stories from the dwarfs. And after burying Strom. My mind replayed the image of his mangled face. The fear I felt was replaced with anger and determination.

"Okay," I said resolutely, "I will try whatever I can."

Qidira threw her arms around my neck. "Thank you." She gave a few gulping, weepy sighs and sat back against the pillows. "So," she asked Ignacia, "when do we start?"

TINCTURE OF JASMINE

*I*gnacia gathered our drying clothes and placed them in a woven bag. She then retrieved a key from a hidden pocket in her robes, unlocked the small wooden door next to the fireplace, and, with a twinkle in her eyes, invited us to follow her into the dark beyond. I had to bend over to get through. Actually, Qidira and Ignacia had to bend over to get through, I had to practically crawl.

The door led to a tunnel a few feet long, and the tunnel opened onto a platform at the top of stone stairs, which ran down into a dark, deep cavern.

I whispered to Qidira, "Didn't we just make it out of the mountains?"

"We did," she whispered back.

Wind whipped through the darkness. Somewhere nearby water dripped. I heard the flutter of wings draw close and ducked as whatever it was zoomed past my ear.

"What was that?" As I ducked to avoid whatever it was that flew over us, I stepped too close to the edge of the small platform. Ignacia grabbed my arm to steady me, keeping me from teetering on the edge of the stone ledge.

"There are creatures who live in these caverns who even we do not understand. I believe, however, that your new friend is a bat." She nodded towards a nearby stalactite, which hung ominously near my left ear. There, closer than I had been aware, a small animal hung from its clawed feet. Bright eyes blinked at me and I swore I saw the glint of sharp fangs as the winged creature flashed a smile.

"Uh . . ." I smiled back.

As if my sociable expression marked acquiescence to his presence, the bat alighted onto my shoulder with but one flap of his leathery wings.

"Aw, it likes you." Qidira reached up and stroked between the animal's ears. He closed his eyes and I felt a hum through his feet into my shoulder where he sat.

"Oh, my Gods, Qid. I think he's purring."

"How do you know it's a he?" she asked.

I looked the small being over. "I don't know, his eyes?"

Qidira peered at the lower portion of the bat. She squinted and pursed her lips. "Do bats even have . . ."

"He's a boy, okay? Trust me."

Ignacia smiled. It was then that I saw from where the small amount of light in which we were bathed was emanating. Ignacia's eyes glowed a soothing blue, casting shadows around us. When she blinked, the light extinguished.

"Oh, now that's cool," I said.

Qidira stood on her tiptoes and inspected my eyes. "Yours are not glowing. Maybe you don't have that part of the ocean sprite power."

"One can never be sure about another's powers," Ignacia crooned. "Follow me."

Again, she beckoned us to pass behind her. We carefully picked our way down the stone stairs, trying not to look into the darkness below. At one point, I slipped and sent a shower of stones into the chasm below. I waited a few, long breaths to hear them hit the bottom, wherever it might be, but all I heard was my own heart pounding inside my chest.

"What's down there?" I asked my new friend, who remained perched on my shoulder. Not expecting an answer, I jumped when he chirped a low vocalization in response. "Do you understand me?" I swear I saw a frown on his face as he flashed a distinctly Qidira-esque glare, crossed his wings, and turned his head away from me. "Okay, I will take that as a yes."

"Elon, come on," Qidira called to me from the bottom of the stairs.

I hurried after them. When I reached the bottom, I saw another small, wooden door set into the rock. Ignacia removed yet another key from her pocket and the sound of the old key in the metal lock echoed around the hushed space. Soon, warm yellow light spilled over us.

We entered a round room that held a bed similar to those we slept on the night before. Spaced evenly around the room were three exits: one to our left, one directly across from us, and then one to the right. Flickering lanterns hung from hooks on the wall. I could see into the room across from us and it looked to be a sitting or dining room. Behind a carved table was yet another wooden door. This one was thick and appeared to be the way out.

Ignacia led us to the left and through a flowing curtain. This space was some kind of spiritual shrine. Carved on the floor was a replica of the mosaic in the main hall of Truth, only this one was simply made of the stone of the floor. The walls were lined with bookshelves, which were covered with old parchment, candles, and bottles of different colored liquids. Baskets of fresh herbs and jars were tucked among the other items. Against the left wall was an elaborately carved couch, the pillow of which was covered with red velvet. Qidira instantly pranced to the seat and settled in.

Along the back wall was a small stone altar. There, flowers, shells, and candles surrounded a smooth wooden carving of a sun. In front of the altar, pillows were scattered around the floor. It reminded me of home and made me smile.

Standing at the shelves, Ignacia picked through the bottles and handed me a small one filled with pearlescent fluid. She took a moment and scratched the bat, who, like a cat settles down in a patch of sunlight, had made himself comfortable on my shoulder. I swirled the flask and then remembered what happened the last time I messed with an unknown substance. I quickly set the bottle back down on the shelf.

"No," Ignacia said, "drink it."

She urged the bottle into my hand and then up to my mouth. I hesitantly let it touch my lips. The thick liquid was smooth. My tongue retrieved a stray drop and it tasted like the smell of the flowers in our living room. After an encouraging nod from Qidira, I drained the swirling fluid.

It warmed me instantly, and I felt it spread steadily across my belly and chest. As it went, the warmth filled my arms and legs. The last place it touched was my head, and I swayed.

"Should I be sitting down?" I asked, moving to Qidira.

"Perhaps, if you are sensitive to it." Ignacia laughed and walked back to the curtained door. "Come now, we have to get you further into the rock." She motioned for us to follow her.

As we went, Qidira stayed next to me to ensure I did not fall. We crossed the main room where the beds were and entered a small alcove that mirrored the herb and shrine room. This space, however, was not warm and fuzzy at all. The floor was covered in patches of loose dirt. The wall was broken by large roots, and the resultant disruption left boulders and tree debris scattered around the area. It looked like the wall had fallen in and no one bothered to clean it up.

"My own little safety precaution," Ignacia said with a sparkle in her now calm blue eyes. "My dear," she said to Qidira, "would you like to do the honors?"

"Me? Elon is the strong one, she can help you."

Ignacia chuckled. "Yes, but you are the fairy. Do you want to practice your fairy magic? I can show you how."

Qidira's face lit up with excitement. "Oh yes, please."

Ignacia turned and left the room. She returned quickly with a vial of clear liquid.

"This one you do not want to swirl," she said, winking at me. "Now Qidira, here is what you will do. Drink this, it will amplify your powers. Then I need you to call to the roots among the stones." She pointed at small brown tufts of vegetation I had not seen. "Call to them to come to you and grow. I cannot tell you exactly how to contact your powers, but I find closing my eyes helps me."

Qidira drank the liquid in one gulp and closed her eyes. I saw her breathe and move her head back and forth. Finally, she opened her eyes.

"I'm getting nothing," she said to Ignacia.

"Let's try this. I'm assuming you have plants at home?"

"Yes," Qidira replied.

"Think about tending to them; think about the connection you feel with them when you care for them."

I chuckled. I was thinking of how Qidira took care of

her plants at home: she always talked to them, touched them, and bathed their individual leaves. I thought this was just a delightful eccentricity, but apparently, it was simply an expression of her fairy heritage.

"Okay. Let me try again," Qidira said

At first, she just stood there, but then she held her hands out to her side, palms facing away from her, fingers splayed wide. Gradually, dirt fell from the rocks, and there was quivering amid the debris.

All of a sudden, my head swam and I had to sit down on one of the larger rocks. "Whoa. Wherever we are going, we might want to get there quickly" Then, after a reproachful look from Qidira, I added, "No pressure."

The creature on my shoulder launched from his perch and fluttered around my head. "Oh, come on buddy," I said. "That's not helping. Now I just want to puke."

The animal zipped back to my shoulder. Once seated, he nipped my earlobe.

"Hey!"

A low-pitched trill sounded near my ear. It filled my head and helped settle my stomach.

"Wow, thanks," I said. I reached up with my opposite hand and pet between his ears, after which more purring ensued.

Across the small space, Qidira released a huff of frustration.

"Don't worry," Ignacia reassured her, "just keep going. You are doing great."

Qidira closed her eyes again. Not long after, the roots began moving the boulders out of the way. Soon, an opening appeared and green vines snaked their way through gaps in the rock, helping the roots with their job. Before long there was a clear path through the wall. Qidira opened one eye and when she saw what she had done, she jumped up and down clapping her hands in excitement. I clapped with her. The bat squeaked.

The room in front of us was as large as the jagged cavern in the main part of Truth. Soft grass carpeted the area and large, twisted trees lined the edges of the room. The trunks were so dense that I could not quite make out the wall. The wood of the trees appeared half in the rock and half out. They reminded me of the trees that lived at the edge of the marsh. Their smooth, tan bark extended to the roots that started well above the ground.

Broad, shiny green leaves swayed over us and when I looked up, I saw a distant point of light high above. Growing in patches at the base of the trees was a myriad of flowers and herbs. Winding their way up a few of the trunks was the same plant we had in our house: jasmine. The smell reminded me again of home and this time it did not cloud my mind.

In front of us, a quick, blue-green stream split the room in half. The water flowed out from between the roots of one of the trees and disappeared beneath the roots of another on the other side. The water was clearly the same as that which flowed through Truth. A wooden bridge with elegantly carved railings invited us to pass over the swirling stream to the other side of the wooded cavern. We followed Ignacia through ankle-deep grass and, once on the bridge, movement in the water caught my eye.

"Water pixies," Ignacia said. "And a couple of new sprites, I think." She leaned over the railing with her brow furrowed. Straightening back up, she said, "The trees seem healthier than normal"—she waved around the room— "I can only assume we have been blessed with a family of tree sprites. Plus"—she pointed toward one of the taller trees— "I think I see the beginnings of a tree-house being built. That would be lovely." She smiled.

I must have been dawdling because Qidira gave me a gentle push as I stalled over the water. As I went, the bat flew up towards the light, rising in tightening spirals.

"Aw, I kind of liked him," I said, craning my neck to follow his flight through the leaves. Soon, however, his fluttering black wings were lost among the foliage. "Oh well."

Ignacia was already on the other side of the room, where she stood, hidden between the trunks of two particularly large trees. There, the opening to a narrow tunnel lay veiled by low-lying greenery. Again, she beckoned us to follow her. We hastened our steps, straining our necks in order to take in the amazing room. When we reached the passageway, I took one last glance behind us, partially hoping my bat friend would return. The opening through which we had entered the forest space was already re-sealed, and, from where we were, I could not make out where it had been; the once open wall was covered with trees again. It made me wonder if there were other, similar doors around the room leading to other places.

After we stepped through the small, rough entrance to a new burrow, the wall sealed behind us. Ignacia's eyes provided some light, but I soon found myself laid out on the rock floor, compliments of a stray root.

Qidira chortled.

"Quiet, you," I said, laughing.

"Here." She bent down and helped me up. "Being that high off the ground must make it difficult to stay upright sometimes, I'm sure."

I just shook my head, my mirth settling over me with comforting assurance, as she hurried to catch up with Ignacia.

We wound our way through dark tunnels like the ones we originally encountered when we entered Truth. The deeper we went, the warmer it got and I tied my outer sweater around my waist. After a dizzying descent, we emerged into a small, natural cavern with projections up from the floor and down from the ceiling. It was similar to the room in which we had bathed only there was not as much blue water. Some of the rock formations ended sharply while others were blunt, with pools of water in them, steaming like a bowl on a pedestal. Some of the water was bubbling, and some spilled over the edge onto the floor.

"This is one of the springs. It is connected to our heat source," Ignacia said.

"That I don't doubt." I fanned my face with my hand. From behind one of the larger water-topped stalagmites, I heard Qidira laugh.

"There." Ignacia pointed across the room to a natural recess in the rock. It resembled a table or a bed. "Lay down over there."

I wove through the rock structures and lay down on the flat surface. Feeling fatigue set in, I closed my eyes. Now still, my body gave into the emotional and physical exertion I had been though in the day. That, and the tincture of jasmine, meant my head soon swam as fog settled over my brain.

"The tincture of night-blooming jasmine I gave you will make you sleepy and cloud your inhibitions. This will help to keep your self-doubt in check," Ignacia said.

"I think I'm already feeling that part," I murmured.

Qidira snorted. It echoed around the cavern. "Sorry, but if I had known it was that easy to address her self-doubt, I would have done so a long time ago."

"Quiet," I shot back.

"Just relax," Ignacia crooned. "The rest is up to you."

I lay on the warm stone, trying to remember how I had originally accessed the ship in the marsh. I was not feeling anything and then I remembered I had been facing the hull. I flipped over. Lifting my arms over my head, I opened my fingers and rested my cheek on the stone. I breathed in and out, slowly and deeply. I tried to project my psychic fingers into the rock below me. Thoughts of this being silly flit through my head, but that's all they were, thoughts; there was none of the self-consciousness I felt in the marsh.

At first, the progression was slow. I felt down into the rock, but when I did not encounter anything in that direction, I sat up and pressed against the rough surface of the niche's wall. I projected my mind deep through the layers.

I jumped when I first came across people. While the sudden appearance of energy surprised me, I did not pull away. I was in a tunnel and beings were walking through my path. I continued reaching into the rock on the other side of the trail. I came to a large room with water and many, different energies.

I must be in the jagged cavern. I felt around. It was a strange, invasive feeling. I wondered if they knew I was there. A few times the beings felt warmer or more alive, and I could even hear the thoughts of a few of them.

I knew I was not going to find what I needed in Truth, so I backed up and tried a different direction. I raised my hands, pressing them against the rock above me and soon something pulled me, like a psychic light at the end of a tunnel.

I followed the feeling.

Before long, I was in a smaller, low ceilinged room full of at least fifteen different entities. They were Other. I felt the Sidar and I knew they felt me as well. Barriers went up and their thoughts were blocked from me. A flurry of activity ensued and the room started to clear. Maybe these were the Untraceables. There were definitely Sidar Other among them, and they definitely did not want me near them.

"I think I found them," I cried.

"Keep going," Ignacia urged. "See what else is there."

I did as she suggested. I left the room where the gathering had been. As I progressed, I felt a few of them again in tunnels that I crossed. I decided to try and follow one of the passageways. I turned my energy down one of the open spaces. It did not seem to be going anywhere and I thought, *the way these tunnels are I could follow it for miles*, so I stopped and went back into the rock.

I tried looking for the guiding-light feeling again, but I could not find it. Exhaustion began to overwhelm me. My barriers faltered and soon a familiar dark caress stroked my energy.

"We've been looking for you . . ."

The voice sounded in my head, like oil oozing from underground. Panic filled my mind. My barriers flew into place before I was even fully aware of the situation and the path of energy I was extending quickly pulled back through the rock and across the rooms. I opened my eyes and once again felt the odd sensation of emptiness.

Qidira saw my eyes fly open and as I bolted upright, she asked, "You found them? Where are they?"

I nodded, jumping from the rock table. "I think I did. Unfortunately, however, I think something else found me as well."

AADNON

*G*ain, we wound through the mountain, and again I lost track of where we had been. A couple of times I reached out my hand and touched the rock as we went, sending energy into the wall. I needed to perfect my new power, but it was exhausting and I was afraid I might once again contact the malevolent invaders, wherever they might be. Still, I now had practice and felt I understood how to activate the ability. Hopefully, if we needed it, I would be able to use my power on command.

The tunnel we were following abruptly stopped at an orange-cream colored stone ladder going up. Ignacia led the way and we found ourselves climbing out of one of the scallop shell rock formations, into the main cavern of Truth.

"I leave you here," Ignacia said. "I need to speak with Aadrick." She hugged us. "Thank you both for trusting me. Thank you for visiting me and allowing me to help you." She bowed and I did not know how to respond.

"You're welcome," was what I finally decided on. That

sounded ungrateful, so I added, "Thank you for everything."

Ignacia smiled and turned to Qidira. "Qidira, thank you for trying your fairy powers. They are definitely in good working order. I have no doubt that as you explore them you will find their full potential."

She faced me again and took both of my hands in hers. "Elon, you are so strong, in both mind and body. You are the one who can do this, and you need to do it your way. Remember, don't lose *your* way."

Ahh, I thought, *that's what everyone means when they keep saying that.*

"Thank you for helping me see my powers, thank you for revealing another part of my heritage to me. You were right, I feel stronger now that I have a new part of myself to explore and embrace." We hugged again and, with a wave, she disappeared through the heavy double doors that led to the meeting hall.

"What now?" I asked Qidira.

"Oh, I know what now." She resolutely set off across the hall toward our sleeping quarters.

I followed her up into our bedroom. I fell heavily onto my mattress and watched as Qidira paced.

"Okay, Qid, stop it. You're making me dizzy. What is it?"

"I am waiting for that girl to show up. She seems to always find us, so I am waiting for her to do so." She folded her arms tightly against her chest.

She was right though, for not a moment after she finished speaking, we heard the dull knock on the rock wall down the steps.

Her affect cold, Qidira said, "Come in."

Tisa entered the room, her head hung. She was holding her hands together in front of her. "I am so sorry I did not tell you," she managed. She ventured a look up and Qidira cocked a hip to one side. Tisa quickly looked back down. But then Qidira threw her arms around the girl and hugged her.

"Oh, you silly child. Of course, you should have told me, but"—she tightened her embrace around the dark-haired girl— "I'm just so happy to meet you." She pulled Tisa over to the other bed and they sat down.

I got up and walked toward the stairs. "I, uh, I'm going to find some food. I'll give you time alone." Qidira just looked at me, smiled, and nodded; she was too busy smoothing Tisa's hair away from her face to comment.

I trotted down the stairs and stood in the jagged cavern. I really did not have the first idea where to find food. I was not in the mood to meet anyone new, so I knew I could not hang around here for very long. I decided to start with Aadrick.

I knocked on the double wooden doors of the main hall and instantly they flew open. A small female dwarf ushered me in and I saw the three brothers, Aadrick's grandsons, seated at a table along the left wall with two females I did not recognize. They were enjoying their lunch.

Perfect, I thought, *just in time.*

"I'm sorry to intrude. Do you mind if I join you?"

The one I recognized as Aadnon jumped up and offered me his seat.

I stepped back, holding my palms up toward the now standing dwarf. "Oh no, I don't want to kick you out of your seat, really. I just thought, perhaps"—I looked towards an empty stretch of bench— "I could just join the party."

"My dear, it is no bother." His smile was warm. "However, if it troubles you, would you care to join me over here?" He motioned to the table on the other side of the room. Surprised, I looked at the remaining two brothers, who quickly looked down at their food.

"Please, don't worry about them. I am chronically the third wheel anyway. These two lovely ladies"—he indicated the women— "are my sisters-in-law. Ladies, this is Elon."

We exchange pleasantries and as we were about to reach the point in the conversation when I might be faced with questions about my heritage, the dwarf woman who let me in to the room returned carrying a tray loaded with another plate of food and a goblet of grape juice. Aadnon rested a hand on the back of my elbow and led me to the other table. I tried to fight it, but was unable; his touch triggered me to glance from him, to my arm, back to him. I tried to pass it off as pure surprise.

He sat at the side of the table and offered me the end seat so that I had a view down the hall to the doors. The young woman set the food and drink in front of me.

"Thank you," I said. She responded with a pleasant smile.

The crisp aroma of fresh lettuce mingled with a rich, savory smell. My stomach churned and I realized how hungry I was. With the first bite, I closed my eyes and smiled. The salad was made up of different types of greens, with sweet cheese crumbled over a warm portion of fish. On the side was a steaming roll and a smaller plate nearby held some of the same fruit we had been served at breakfast. The grape juice was cold and just strong enough to make me want more.

I looked up and saw Aadnon watching me.

"What?" I asked self-consciously.

He smiled. "You are very beautiful. Your hair is like woven rays of sunshine and your eyes . . . they are like the sea."

"Um . . . thank you." I was not used to compliments.

I sank my fork back into the food and then remembered I needed to say a blessing. I bowed my head before uttering my normal expression of gratitude for food, "Itadakimasu." When I was done, I retrieved the fork rather clumsily and in doing so flung a piece of cheese at Aadnon.

"Oh no! I'm so sorry." I reached over and tried to brush the crumble from the arm of his velvet jacket. The green material was so soft, however, that I only succeeded in smearing the cheese into the fabric. I tried again with my napkin, but we ended up bumping arms, and my hand got tangled in his elbow as he tried to move it. I withdrew my arm with nervous laughter and decided it was better to keep my hands to myself. "Sorry," I muttered again.

"No worries," he said, still smiling. "The cheese has a mind of its own." When he was done resettling himself, a pregnant silence ensued. He cleared his throat, and I managed a sip of grape juice without spilling it all over my lap.

Usually, when there was a silence that I did not want turning into a question session about me, my best approach was to ask about the other person. People love to talk about themselves; I could say nothing in the entire conversation and walk away with the other person loving me, simply because I asked them questions, and then listened to the answers.

"So, tell me," I began, "aren't you the oldest son? That puts you second in line for the throne, no?" I took a bite of the crisp salad.

He chuckled. "I am fourth in line, actually, but do you really want to talk about my place in the lineage?"

Legitimately curious now, I said, "Well, now that you've said that, yeah, I do." I wiped my mouth on my napkin.

"Fourth? You're not the oldest? I just assumed based on how people were sitting at the table . . ."

"I am the oldest, but after my father succeeds my grandfather, Aaldin will be the next eventual successor." He was still smiling, so I assumed that was not a bad thing.

"Do you mind me asking why that is?"

"No, I don't mind." He relaxed back into his chair. "It is a little personal, so I apologize in advance if I reveal more than perhaps you were looking for. I do not want to offend or embarrass you."

I laughed at this. "There is next to nothing I don't talk about, so no worries. It takes a lot to offend me, but believe me, if it happens, you'll know."

He executed a small nod of understanding and continued, "I did not want to have children."

"That's it? No kids so no crown?"

"Sort of. No kids, no heirs; and while my brothers' children would therefore naturally fall as the heirs to the throne, it's odd to have a single king. What is a king without his queen?" There was a quick sparkle in his eyes. "I also wanted to be free to follow other pursuits. As my grandfather said, I am of a curious nature. I wanted to be free to travel, to explore if I needed to. I could not do that with the responsibilities of king weighing on me. I wanted to do what was right for the people, and I just did not think that a reluctant king with wanderlust was the best thing for Truth."

I was impressed with his honesty and integrity.

He continued, "And now that you have tried, successfully for a few moments, to divert the conversation away from you, let's talk about you."

Oh, I liked this guy.

"Sure, but first," I said, leaning toward him, "can we talk about the weaponry Aadrick mentioned?" I felt like an impatient child at solstice time, waiting for a present that I felt guilty for even expecting.

His eyes widened an almost undetectable amount.

"What?" I said quickly, sitting up straight. "Did I say something wrong?"

"Oh no," he replied, reaching out and touching my hand. Again, I glanced down in surprise at his touch. "No, no," he continued, "it was your eyes, they shifted color. I've seen it a few times, mostly with Ignacia. It just surprised me, that's all."

"Oh," I said, self-conscious yet again.

He must have been able to tell that I was uncomfortable because he quickly added, "But of course, we can talk about it, if you would like. Actually, when you are done eating, we can go down to the forge. Would you like that?"

Again, I felt childlike in the eagerness of my reply, "Yes, very much."

"Then I will let you eat and I will return soon."

He stood and pushed the bench back under the table. He hesitated, one hand resting on the table, looking at me. From this distance, his royal blue eyes shone like stars. I did not flinch or shift because his gaze was not at all uncomfortable.

"Until then," he finally said. He bowed and walked away. I watched him all the way out of the door.

AULDE

J finished every bit of my food and drink. By the time I was done, the others had finished as well and had left in pairs, coming over to say their goodbyes in turn. I got up and strolled down the hall, looking at each of the tapestries. I would stare at the wall next to the images and was able to catch movement in each one.

Along one wall of the room was a light-colored fabric woven with images of a woman smiling at the sky. She was surrounded by small flying creatures. Her entire being was beautiful, with blue eyes, and long, wheat-colored hair that blended with the sunlight such that I could not differentiate where one ended and the other began. She was slender and it was not clear if she was a dwarf, as there was nothing near her to provide a frame of reference for her size. She seemed more fragile than a dwarf and, try as I may, I could not place her heritage. Out of the corner of my eye, I saw the wings on the small creatures move, and I saw the woman's chest rise with a sigh. I looked directly at the image and was taken by her beauty.

"Intoxicating," Aadnon said at my elbow. I jumped and hopped to the side.

"I'm sorry," he said, palms loosely facing out toward me in a gesture of disarming reassurance. "I did not mean to startle you."

"No, it's okay," I said, bringing my feet back under me. I turned to the weaving again. "Who is she?"

"Sarina, Mother of the Fairies. Even the image of her is entrancing. She is beautiful, no?"

"Yes."

We stood looking at the image for a few moments before Aadnon gestured toward the exit. "Shall we?"

I smiled and mirrored his motions. "After you."

His face lit up with a whimsical smile and he said, "Of course."

He led me out of the hall and toward the great stairs. He took a torch from the wall and we passed through the small wooden door to the left of the grand stairwell. The tunnel we found ourselves in was warmer than even the main hall and it instantly began sloping downwards.

We moved downwards in silence. I don't know for how long we walked, but it was a downhill slope the entire way. Just when I thought our descent would never end, I saw an opening ahead of us that was filled with flickering firelight. I heard the sharp noises of metal work and soon I was standing on a platform overlooking a natural cavern much like the one in which I had attempted to find the Sidar, only exponentially bigger. The floor had various tiers, the lowest of which was a platform extending over running water. The room was almost uncomfortably warm and I assumed this was one of the geothermal sources of heat for the settlement.

We took stairs carved into the wall down to a mid-tier out-cropping that appeared to be the main floor of the operation. I looked around the area and saw recesses carved out of the walls that contained boiling water. I walked to one and found a hollow tunnel extending up into the ceiling of each recess.

Scattered around the platform flames crackled in fire circles or ovens. Every forge was situated next to a natural pool of water. There were dwarfs of all sizes hammering on metal. A couple stopped to look at us, while others simply glanced over and continued their work.

Aadnon approached a male dwarf in a leather apron who was inspecting weaponry. They embraced and Aadnon spoke something into his ear before making introductions.

"Elon, this is Aulde, he is one of my cousins. He has the gift of metallurgy."

I shook his hand, which seemed to amuse him. "Nice to meet you."

The jovial, bearded dwarf looked me up and down. As he walked around me, he said, "And you, young lady, need no introduction." When he returned to his original position in front of me, he nodded at Aadnon, shook my hand again, and went to speak with another dwarf.

"What do you think?" Aadnon asked.

"I think it is amazing." I turned around where I stood, taking in the height of the room, and the red color of the rock. "Do you all really need all of these weapons, or is this a beefing up of your arsenal due to the vamphyres?"

"The vamphyres. Should something happen, we will all need not only weapons but armor as well. We are also crafting weapons for the Sidar"—from a nearby table he picked up a small chain with a jagged ball at either end and offered it to me— "if they will take them."

What he handed me looked more like a trinket than a weapon, but when I took it from him it fell in my hand with disproportionate weight. I almost dropped it because I was fooled by its size.

"What are these?" I asked, feeling the length of the chain. "Wait," I said, "don't tell me, I want to try." I held one of the weighted ends and swung the other above my head, around and around in quickening circles. I found a nearby rocky projection by which no one was standing and let loose the weapon. It did what I hoped it would: it encircled the top, its two ends entwining, and cut off the top of the orange rock.

Aadnon appeared pleased. When I retrieved the weapon and handed it back to him, he said, "You keep it, it's yours now. It might not work as well for another."

I slipped the metal into my pocket where it settled comfortably against my leg.

"Have you seen enough, or would you like to see more?" he asked.

"Thank you, I think I've seen enough." I ran my hands along the rest of the weapons lying on the table. "Besides, it's very warm down here." I turned to him. "I don't think I am appropriately dressed for this occasion."

"I think you are perfectly dressed for any occasion." A comforting smile shone on his face.

"Thank you," I responded, returning his smile as my cheeks flushed from more than just the temperature.

"But it is getting late and I can imagine you would like to reunite with Madame Qidira. I will take you to her."

I was relieved when we finally stepped into the main hall as the heat had been uncomfortable. I do not sweat as much as others do and if I am not careful, I can easily suffer from hyperthermia.

Aadnon led me across the jagged cavern and, at the bottom of the stairs to my room, he stopped.

"I know it is a confusing time for you right now, Elon," he said.

"A little, I suppose. It's less confusing than it is expectant, I guess, and I tend to get in trouble if I think about what to expect. Things turn out better if I just do the doing part."

"I understand. Sometimes it is easier to not think too much and just do the next thing in front of you."

This expressed my sentiments exactly and I smiled. "It's nearly *always* simpler to just do the next thing in front of you. But while it might be simpler, it's not always the *easiest* thing to do. Most times, for me at least, I get all bogged down with thinking about what it is going to look like, what *should* I do, what's the right thing, what if something goes wrong, what *if* . . . blah, blah, blah." I smiled, thinking about how Qidira dealt with my *what ifs*. She patiently let me visit every permutation until I was done. It must drive her crazy. "It can be paralyzing, and then nothing gets done."

"What are you afraid of?" he asked.

His bold question caught me off guard. My mind flashed back to what I had seen in the star basin. I was not ready to talk about any of that yet.

I shrugged and said, "Tons of things, I suppose."

"Vague answer," he said, "but that's okay."

"It's not so important at this moment what it is I'm scared of, just how I respond to my fear. I think it is better for me to not think and just do."

"Fair enough," he responded with a nod. "On a slightly more official note, do you have any idea when you might be headed to find the Sidar?"

"I think soon." I thought about how anxious Qidira must be just sitting around, and I myself was starting to feel the need to move on. There was momentum in our plan now and I thought it was probably a good idea to follow it. "Perhaps in the morning."

"I know my father and grandfather would like to see you off. I will tell them of your intentions and we will have breakfast waiting for you in the main hall when you awake."

"Alright." I smiled, partially at the thought of leaving, but mostly in response to the idea of seeing him again. I shifted uncomfortably.

He squared his shoulders, took one of my hands, and brushed his lips over the back of it. His skin was velvety against mine and I was grateful that my cheeks were already flushed from the heat of the forge.

"Until then," he said, releasing my hand. With one final smile, he turned to walk away. When he got to the double wooden doors he turned back around. Suddenly self-conscious that he had caught me watching him, I smiled and hurried up the stairs

When I reached the top, Qidira was alone, packing.

"How was it with Tisa?" I asked, sitting at the table.

"Wonderful," she replied. "I could not be happier with my daughter-in-law. She is sassy, huh? I like that."

"Yeah, she'll fit right in." I let Qidira gush. She talked about Tisa and relayed the story of how she and Tariq met, their wedding next to the lake, and about Tisa's heritage.

"She might come in handy, the whole forest troll thing," Qidira said, placing folded clothes into her bag. Finally, she turned to me, "What did you do while you were gone?"

I told her about lunch and the trip to what felt like the center of the mountain. I showed her the bi-weighted weapon and told her the dwarfs were making them for the Sidar. It was warm when I reached for it and did not cool once out of my pocket. Qidira took it from me, looked it over, and handed it back to me.

"That's yours now," she said, "no one else will be able to use it."

"Aadnon said something similar." I took the weapon back and looked down at it. It settled into my palm.

"Dwarf metal-magic, remember? You are Sidar, that magic is specific to you, and now that it has chosen you, well, it is yours."

"Huh." I considered the weapon and then slipped it back into my pocket. Again, it felt comforting against my leg.

Not long after, Tisa entered the room with a tray of food. This time she joined us for the meal. Our dinner was a steaming, creamy soup and more of the same delightful grape juice I had before. We ate slowly, enjoying light conversation about what life was like in the marsh.

When we were done, I told them both about breakfast in the morning.

Tisa's face fell. "You are leaving in the morning then?"

"I think so," I said, sipping grape juice and looking at Qidira for input.

"Tisa, you of all people must know how badly I want to find Tariq." She smiled and reached for the girl's hands. "I will bring him back when I can."

We both knew she was making a potentially empty promise, as our journey might not turn out well for anyone. Tisa nodded. Her reluctance at letting go of Qidira was apparent.

"I will continue to wait." She sighed.

Qidira leaned over and gave her a hug. I got up and went into the bathroom, washed my face, and changed for bed. When I returned, Tisa was gathering the dishes and soon, with a kiss for both of us, she left down the stairs.

I hugged Qidira. "I'm scared." I admitted.

"Me, too," she replied. "But it is going to be alright. Whatever happens, it is going to be alright."

I knew she was right, but I still could not settle the growing feeling of unease in my gut.

SHIRAH

$\mathcal{I}$ meditated before bed. At first, I tried to sort through all of the things I had learned since leaving our house, especially what I discovered since arriving here. After I ran through events, I tried to clear my mind. The real purpose of the meditation was to try and reach out to the Sidar. While I had never had full contact with them while awake before, I thought I might try. If it did not work, I was hoping I might get myself relaxed enough to reach them in my sleep.

I sat on the floor with my back to the bed for at least a couple thousand breaths. I concentrated on my breathing, but every time I tried to extend myself outwards it did not work. But I continued to breathe, and I tried to free my mind of thoughts, bringing myself back to my breathing pattern.

I am not the world's best meditator, but my parents taught me that any time spent being quiet with myself was a good thing, so I continued to try. Try as I may, however, I found myself dozing off.

"Just go to sleep already," Qidira muttered from amidst her fluffy bedding. "They will come to you then."

She was right. I do not even remember lying down. I just remember feeling as though I was being woken up, only I was no longer in my safe niche in Truth; I was standing next to the lake outside. I waited for the cold, but it did not come. The stars were bright, winking at me from the black blanket that surrounded the full, blue moon. The air was sweet with the scent of new growth, and there was a Sidar woman next to me.

She looked out over the water and spoke without turning toward me. "It is beautiful here, so big and yet so quiet."

I watched her as she smiled and breathed in the night air. She was more human than the other Sidar I had seen in my dreams. Finally, she turned and took my hands in hers.

I waited to hear her voice in my mind, but she spoke aloud. "Elon, thank you for coming." Her face warm and open. "I am Shirah. I am a human-Sidar Other who has joined the sect here on Palus."

"Hi," I responded lamely.

"I know it has not been easy, but I also know that we were right to ask for your help." She squeezed my fingers. "Sleep well tonight. We will send you a restful mind, and I will be there for you in the morning." I nodded. "We know that you found the direction in which to start out for us—"

"I did?"

She smiled. "When you searched through the rocks. Do you not remember feeling the pull?"

"I . . ." I stumbled over sharing about the dark energy. "I do remember."

"We also know that you may have found the Vandals, or,

as the dwarfs call them, the Untraceables. We understand that the woman you have with you is the mother of one of these nomads, and we cannot have them finding us. I am sorry."

"I can't look for Tariq?" I asked, eyes widening.

She shook her head.

"He is part Sidar," I responded, supplication for assistance ringing in my voice.

"I know him, and he is half Sidar in fact. We wished for him to stay with us, but"—she shrugged— "he found love and chose to stay with the dwarfs instead. We do not begrudge anyone happiness outside of the sect; communal living can be difficult."

She dropped my hands and moved to the water. Kneeling, she placed her palms on the surface of the still lake. Moonlight danced on the resultant ripples, which moved out from where she interrupted the glassy calm. She closed her eyes and was still. I did not know what she was doing, but I hoped it was something to do with Tariq. I was annoyed that she was asking me not to look for him, and I hoped she had another idea.

Finally, she stood up, wiping her hands on the legs of her cotton pants. "Once we arrive in Laet, our home, the elders have agreed to contact him and see if he will come home."

"Thank you," I replied. Relief washed through me. I couldn't imagine the fire storm that would ensue if I had to tell Qidira that we were no longer going to look for her son.

"Elon, again, thank you. Go now and sleep. Everything will be well in the morning and we will meet again." We embraced, and as she moved away, I fell through familiar fog and found myself staring at the shifting water above my bed back in Truth. I spent only a moment pondering what had just happened and soon I was fast asleep. I did not dream or stir for the rest of the night.

When I awoke the next morning, the sun was shining through the water. A shifting glint across the room caught my eye and, when I looked more closely, I saw a sword lying across my gear. It was encased in a sheath of brown leather and light from above danced on the gilded silver at the tip.

I stumbled out of bed and, rubbing my eyes clear of sleep, picked up the new weapon. Instantly, the weight was comforting and I knew this sword belonged in my hand.

Taking care to avoid the sharp edge, I drew the blade from its casing and held it up in front of me. Images of the ocean were etched into the metal blade. Fish and winged sprites swam among tendrils of seagrass. The silver blade ended at a cross-guard that was more intricate than others I had seen: each side had two water serpents winding around each other, their jaws merging in the middle to form one, toothy mouth, a small tongue gracefully laying along the center.

The tails of the serpents wound around a golden rain guard that held a now familiar image: one large center orb surrounded by three smaller spheres. The Sidra here was made from a blue fire opal that shifted and seemed to burn in the metal. The stone was strong, as if the guard was formed around it.

The hilt was a pale, butter-soft braided leather with golden fibers woven amid the strands. I wrapped my hand around it and found it to be an exact fit for my long fingers. The edge of my hand rested on the stone that created the pommel, a smooth, opaque material that looked like moonstone, with gray amorphous swirls amid an opalescent background. The stone was cool against the edge of my hand

I replaced the weapon into its sheath and picked up the cords of leather folded next to it. It was a back sling, something I had never tried before.

Cool, I thought.

My movements must have woken Qidira because I heard her stir behind me.

"Hmm . . . Elon?" she said in a voice heavy with sleep.

"Yeah, babe." I went to her bed and rubbed her back. "Good morning."

I told her about my interaction with Shirah during the night, but I left out the part about not looking for Tariq. I thought I would breach that later. Amid a titter of uncharacteristic giggles, I showed her my new sword.

"Wow," she exclaimed. "Very nice. You think Aadnon sent it to you?" She gave me a sly smile.

Heat rose across my face. "Yeah, I think he had it made for me."

She handed the sword back to me. "Good. Perhaps his magic will help protect you."

I looked up and saw that her face was solemn. I attempted to lighten the mood. "Nah, Qid, nothing's going to happen to me." I pulled her into a hug. "Who would be around to annoy you if I wasn't here?" She put her arms around my waist.

"So," I said, "Are you ready to restart this crazy mission?"

She made a half-laugh, half-snort kind of noise. "Not now, but after some food and a bath, yeah, I think I am."

"Aadnon said something about food this morning."

"He did, did he . . ." Her eyes sparkled and half of her mouth turned upwards. I poked her in the arm.

"A goodbye breakfast or something."

"Mmm hmm, okay," she responded, stretching from fingers to toes.

She got out of bed and dressed. We decided we would bathe before breakfast, so we grabbed what we needed and headed out. As we enjoyed a glorious bath in the warm springs, I told her more about my time with Aadnon

Shaking her head at me with a knowing smile, she dunked once more under the water. When she came back up, she slicked back her hair, grabbed one of the towels we brought with us, and stepped out. She wrapped herself in the cloth before using an extra towel to dry her hair.

I, too, exited the watery warmth, lingering as long as I could. This might well be the last warm water we saw for a while and I was not anxious to leave. We dressed again in our own clean clothes.

"Come on," I said, "let's go eat."

The tables in the main meeting hall had been pulled away from the walls and there were all manner of dwarfs flanking them, many more than I had seen around Truth. In fact, given the difference in appearance, it appeared as if they had come out of the woodwork. They were of all different heights. Some stood on chairs and still just barely reached the table top. Red, blonde, white, and black hair dotted the crowd, and every eye was on us.

Everyone stopped talking when we entered. We were escorted down the center of the hall, past all of the dwarfs who had already started eating their breakfast but who had paused to watch our entrance.

A smaller, square table sat at the base of the stairs of the platform that held the high council. We were seated and food was placed in front of us. I glanced at Aadnon and he flashed me a sweet smile. I smiled back, my eyes surreptitiously darting to Aadrick, as if he might not approve of public flirting.

Soon after the food was brought to us, the king stood up and addressed the room. "Thank you, everyone, for joining us this morning. We are here to see off our most recent visitors: Elon"—he motioned for me to stand, which I did, and, not knowing what else to do, I waved to the crowd— "and Qidira." Qidira stood up and made a small bow. *Show off*, I mouthed to her.

"I have brought you all here from your various boroughs and clans to introduce you to these two. They are to be your guests, as they have been ours. Do not fear any vamphyre blood that you might sense." A buzz ran through the room, but it quickly died down. "Elon is a friend." He looked at me and smiled. I chanced a quick glance at Aadnon again, hoping he would not be looking at me. To my chagrin, however, he was.

Stupid, I thought, *they are talking about me. Everyone is looking at me, why wouldn't he also?* I quickly looked down at the table.

"Elon," Aadrick continued, "the dwarfs who gathered here today are a sampling of the people who live in these mountains. Wherever your travels take you within this range, there will be dwarf help."

"Thank you," I said sincerely. I turned to the crowd, "And thank you, for the willingness to help us." I was more touched than my voice relayed; tears formed in my eyes.

Aadrick motioned for us to sit, and then he led us in a dwarf blessing. It was an acknowledgment of those who grew the food, and the sprites who helped create the bounty. It was nice, but a little long for my liking. Finally, we were able to eat.

The noise in the room was loud enough that Qidira and I were able to talk over our food as though we were alone. I decided to tell her about the plan to find the Sidar; I told her that Shirah had indicated she would take us to the Sidar and *then* help us to find Tariq. It was kind of true. She seemed to not take it too badly.

"It makes sense," she said, taking in a mouthful of warm, syrupy bread. "We are here to help the Sidar. I want to find Tariq, but I know what our primary goal is." I sighed with relief, then I reached across the table and squeezed her hand.

We were nearing the end of the food on the table and both of us continued to eat, not because we were still hungry but because the food was so good. Suddenly, a hush fell over the room, and I looked up. At first, I turned toward the main doors, but when I saw everyone looking past me, I twisted back to look toward the royals. Standing to the left of the table, joined by Ignacia, was Shirah. She was in a white robe like the ones I had seen on the Sidar in my night time visitations. Her hands were folded in front of her and she was smiling at me.

I leaned across the table and said to Qidira, "That's Shirah."

"She's pretty," Qidira said. "Human?"

"Yeah, partially."

Aarron was on his feet, conversing closely with Shirah. She nodded and, after an intense discourse with the king, came to us.

"Good morning," she said, placing a hand on my arm.

"Good morning," I replied, standing up. "This is Qidira."

"Yes, good morning to you, too." She smiled her warm smile and shook hands with Qidira. "Are you done eating? I don't want to take you away from this feast too soon."

I looked to Qidira who said, "I'm done."

"Me, too," I said.

"Good. Your belongings are out in the main cavern. Shall we?" She motioned in the direction of the double doors.

"After you," I responded.

She bowed and moved on, ahead of us. I glanced over my shoulder at Aadnon and saw him rise from his chair, watching our exit. His face held a barely detectable look of loss. Qidira pulled me by the hand and I turned back toward the doors and followed Shirah out.

Once in the main cavern, we saw Tisa and a few others. Aulde was there, holding the sword. His face beamed like the glowing metal.

"You like it?" His hearty brogue was childlike with excitement.

"I love it," I replied. He bounced on the balls of his feet and I could tell he was anxious to have me try it on.

First, however, Tisa handed me a dark sweater, larger than others given to me during my stay in Truth. "It's cold in the mountains this time of year."

"Thanks." I hugged her.

I pulled the soft garment over my head and walked to Aulde. He turned me around and fed something over my right shoulder, and then around my waist from the left. He turned me back to face him and fastened the leather straps with two clasps. The hooks were silver, worked into the shape of hands. When clasped, they held each other, fingers of one curled around those of the other.

"The clasp is firm." He tugged at the harness. "But if you need to release quickly," he said, pulling on a braided cord hanging from the underside of the hands, "just pull this"—he pulled harder and the hands released— "and the clasp will come undone." The sword began to fall, but someone behind me caught it. I spun quickly to retrieve the weapon, and my hands almost grabbed Aadnon.

"Sorry," I said, taking the sword he offered. "I mean, thanks for the gift. It is exquisite."

"It was my pleasure." I saw on his face that indeed it was. His deep blue eyes watched me without blinking.

They wrinkled at the edges as his smile reached his temples. "I wish I could go with you."

I suddenly felt awkward, as though the thought of him coming with us would be a disaster. I knew my doubt showed on my face because he quickly added, "No, no, don't worry. I am not, nor am I asking to. I simply am saying that you are setting out on an adventure the likes of which I have never experienced. I envy you that."

I relaxed yet still my heart raced at the thought of having him near.

Stop, I instructed myself. *Not now. Sidar first, matters of the heart later.*

"And I envy you your family here," I said.

He chuckled and looked down. "I suppose." His eyes returned to my face. "But family can be hard. I know mine is, especially since there are expectations that were created before I was even born."

"Some family, however, expectations and all, is better than no family." I found myself vulnerable in a way that was uncomfortable. I consciously reined it in. "At least I have Qidira," I said finally.

"Yes, that you do." He looked over his shoulder at where Tisa was helping Qidira put on a new pack that she must have made just for the trip.

"Well," I said, feeling awkward, "thanks again."

"Elon," he said in a soft voice, "if your journey is successful, if you are able in the end, will you return here, please?" I shifted my gaze back and forth between his eyes.

"Yes," I answered, "I will."

LAET

Shirah led us through the jagged cavern to the far upper corner, where, hidden behind a large outcropping of rock, a heavy wooden door stood open. The safety precautions were impressive, with weighty bolted locks on both sides. Before she passed through the doorway, Qidira gave a final wave to the crowd that was still watching us. Then, with a final look around the room, and a last smile at Aadnon, I followed her.

The first few feet of the tunnel were similar to the dwarf tunnels we had been traveling in for the last couple of days: firmly packed dirt floor with rough walls and a low ceiling. Within a few steps however the passage changed dramatically—the sides of the tunnel widened and the ceiling became taller until the passageway was perfectly round. The earthen floor disappeared and we were walking on smooth rock. It looked as though someone had come through with a huge drill and hollowed out a flawlessly smooth, geometrically perfect circular tube. I ran my fingers along the wall and found that I could feel through the rock with little effort. I was so fascinated by this that I ran into the back of Qidira where she had stopped.

"Whoops, sorry." I grabbed her shoulders and caught myself up on my toes to keep from falling forward. She laughed. We both looked up and Shirah had turned around to face us. Behind her, the tunnel ended at a smooth granite wall.

"We must pass through," Shirah said.

"Great," I mumbled.

Qidira shushed me. "I'm sure it will be fine," she whispered.

Shirah continued, "I will go through first, but then wait for me to help you through. The wall bars against vamphyres *and* dwarfs unless assisted by a Sidar."

"Take that," I said childishly to Qidira.

She rolled her eyes but looked annoyed all the same; she held her head higher and pursed her lips.

Shirah turned and placed both hands on the stone. She stood like that for a fraction of a breath before she melted through the barrier. We just watched. Within seconds of her full disappearance, two hands reached back for us.

We looked at each other and Qidira grasped the beckoning hands. They pulled her through and soon she, too, was gone. I looked behind me, for what reason I was not sure. When I returned to face the wall, the disembodied hands were there waiting for me. I took them and began my journey through the rock.

This stretch of stone was not nearly as thick as the last one I had come through, but the squeezing sensation was just as uncomfortable. The rock, however, glided over my skin this time, instead of biting into my flesh, and the whole journey seemed to happen relatively quickly. I felt my hands emerge and then the rest of me popped out on the other side. I stumbled but soon regained my balance.

"Was that better?" Qidira asked.

"Yes," I replied, "much." She rubbed the side of my arm vigorously in a gesture of hearty affection.

Shirah flashed her warm smile and we continued down a passage, which looked the same as on the other side: smooth and round. I looked around Shirah to see what was in front of us, but all I saw was more of the same, leading off into darkness. Seeing darkness in front of us made me look around where we stood.

I had not noticed before but there was definitely light around us. I stopped walking and looked everywhere for the source. Shirah had not noticed that I stopped, and as she walked away, I noticed that the light followed her. Still, I was not left standing in darkness. I looked over my body, along my arms, torso, and legs, but still could not find any source of light. Shirah stopped and looked back at me.

She must have noticed my search because she said, "Bioluminescence. The rocks glow when you are near them. It is responding to the Sidar in you."

Qidira looked from one of us to the other and moved back toward me. The light did not follow her. "Well, I guess that settles that once and for all," she said with a smile, "there is no Sidar in me."

"Put your hand on the wall," Shirah gently commanded. Qidira did as she was told and a slight glow spread from where she touched the rock. She pulled her hand back and a faint, blurry impression of a small hand lingered for a moment before disappearing. She rubbed at the hand that had been on the wall and looked toward Shirah.

"When a woman has a child sometimes the blood mingles. Maybe you picked up some of Tariq's blood when he was born?" I postulated.

"Still?" she said, skeptically. "After sixteen years?"

"Apparently, yes," Shirah replied. "Good enough?" Shirah asked.

"Good enough," we both responded.

After much wending and weaving through the round tunnels, we found ourselves at the bottom of a stone spiral staircase. We climbed in what felt like endless dizzying spirals until, finally, my head emerged through a hole in the rock.

I looked around and saw that we were in another circular room, with two openings, one across from the hole in the floor through which we were emerging, and one to our right. The entire room was made of a cream-colored stone, streaked through with brownish-orange veins. Embedded into the rock between the doorways were stairs leading up toward sunlight. Small trees gently swayed above the opening and a soft breeze rustled around the room. The wind smelled of summer and the dew the sun claims when it rises in the morning.

When I put my hands down on the floor the rock felt smooth and soft. I walked a few paces and rubbed my hand along the curve of the wall.

"Soapstone," I said to no one in particular.

"Yes," Shirah replied.

When I turned around, I found we were no longer alone; three other Sidar had silently joined us. They stood in a patch of sunlight, which shone down through the half-open ceiling. The warm rays glinted off of the silver hair of the male and lent a glow to the golden locks of the two females.

I looked up.

"The wind promised snow last week," I mumbled to Qidira. "No way it's this warm now."

She nodded and continued her own scrutiny of what was visible of the level above us. The breeze blew around the room, carrying the assurance of warmth instead of the metallic tang that precedes snow.

"Where—" My question was cut short when a cream-colored four-legged animal emerged from a small archway under the stairs. She padded slowly toward the Sidar, all the while keeping her bright blue eyes on me. She flicked her blue-tipped tail as she stalked across the room. I had never seen one before, but I knew this was a cat. This one looked like it was used to being worshiped.

She wound her way between the legs of the Sidar and then bounded effortlessly up the stairs. I wanted to follow her, to see what was up there, but I refocused on the Sidar in front of me as Shirah introduced us.

"Elon, this is Farzah"—the man bowed— "Azedah, and Sheh." The women bowed in turn. I bowed back and waved. Sheh came out from behind the others, took the pack from my shoulder, and encouraged me to remove my backpack. Similarly, Azedah relieved Qidira of her burden. I heard an unfamiliar voice in my mind, *"Follow us, we will show you to your quarters."*

"Uh, okay," I said aloud.

Qidira, at first confused, said, "It's okay to do the telepathic thing, just as long as you let me know when it has anything to do with me."

"Sorry," Sheh apologized out loud. "We are mostly silent here. I suppose by now it is a habit."

"No, really, it's fine," Qidira replied. "I'm only going to assume you are talking about me if you point and laugh." She smiled. The Sidar smiled as well and we followed them up the stairs and into the sunshine.

Soon, we were standing in the middle of a circular courtyard which was surrounded by two- and three-story high buildings cut from the same stone as the room we just left. Everything was round—the roofs, the doorways, and the stones that made up the floor. Even the small trees, trimmed into perfect spheres, were planted in arcs; there were five semi-circles of trees, each lining the edge of a hole in the ground just like the one we had come through. The architecture was built directly into the side of the mountains. Where the buildings ended the mountains continued to rise; it was like sitting in a cream and orange stone bowl.

The breeze that reached us down below was just as sweet up here. Sunlight touched my face and I looked up, smiling and breathing deeply. It took a moment for the inconsistency to hit me once more.

"Shirah, how is it sunny here? How is it warm?" I asked.

Qidira turned at this as well and asked, "And shouldn't you all be as concerned as the dwarfs, if not more so, about the vamphyres that just arrived? Having an open sky does not seem safe."

Shirah smiled. "It is an energy field, created by the Sidra. Sadly, it is not actually the sun, although the Star does a good job mimicking the sun that warms our home planet. And yes, an open sky would be dangerous, and an invitation to any vamphyre who would dare attempt the dangerous flight through the snowy peaks of the mountains, but if you looked down upon us from the sky all you would see would be fog, just like the other valleys in these hills. The shield is impenetrable, even to us."

"Well," Qidira said, "it's lovely."

We were led across the large courtyard, into which two of our homes could fit, and through an arch into a building. We found ourselves standing in yet another circular room, this one with a vaulted ceiling two stories high. The rooms that ran around the edges of this main space were all open to each other and to the middle area. In the center was a small fountain, a simple well in the floor with a round stone sitting in the middle. Water bubbled happily out of the top and spilled seamlessly over the sphere. The sound of the falling cascade echoed through the room.

Halfway to the ceiling, a balcony ran around the space, with a few arched openings leading off of it. We walked into one of the interconnected rooms and climbed tile stairs to the second floor. Soon we were led into another large area that was, of course, circular, with a domed ceiling. There, piles of brightly colored cushions made from silk and velvet were scattered across two thick mattresses resting on the floor. Azedah and Sheh left our gear next to the beds.

I heard in my head, "*We must go now. Please follow us.*"

"Can we change?" I said out loud, then for Qidira I added, "They say we need to follow them."

"It's warmer here than we expected," Qidira added, "may we change first?"

"Of course," Azedah said out loud. "*Meet us down by the fountain when you are ready, but please, do not take too much time,*" she added telepathically.

"*Sure,*" I relayed back to her. Both women left after a bow, pulling a silk curtain across the doorway as they went.

"So, who do you think stole whose decorating idea?" I asked Qidira, walking to an ornately carved stone table and checking out the decoration.

"My guess?" she replied. "The dwarfs took tips from the Sidar. This room is awfully familiar."

"A bit more lavish, I would say." I leaned closer to look at the carved legs of the table. Like everything else here, it was made from soapstone, set into the wall, with two elaborately crafted legs resting on a woven rug made up of scarlet, blues, and black. It was much like the rug we had at home, one Qidira brought with her down from the mountains.

The legs of the table were carved with images of suns, cats, dragons, and intricate scrolls of stone. It was beautiful, but I got bored just *thinking* about carving all of it. I looked away with admiration for whoever had done the work.

Qidira and I changed into lighter clothes: she into a cotton skirt and me into lighter pants and a looser shirt. I moved my two-headed weapon into my new pants and felt its delight at being back with me. *Morning Star*, I thought. From where it came, I do not know, but that was its name. I shared this with Qidira.

"Not surprising," she said with a smirk.

"What?"

"The name seems to fit and it does not surprise me that you named it—now it is part of the family."

The thought of a new family member made me happy.

"I love you, Qid."

"I love you, too."

EMIR

*W*e joined Azedah and Shah downstairs and they led us back across the courtyard and down another flight of stairs, into yet another subterranean chamber. This room, however, had one of the smooth, round tunnels leading off of the back wall, away from the habitation. Following this, we wove around until we came to yet another wall.

Both Sidar turned to us and I heard one of their voices in my head, "*Wait here, we—*"

I verbally cut her off, "We know; you will go through and reach back for us."

"*Yes,*" she said in my head.

They disappeared through the rock and shortly we were both brought through, as well.

Once on the other side, we found ourselves surrounded by the dark rock that lined the dwarfs' habitat. There, Farzah waited for us with a torch. The five of us continued down the tunnel into a familiar dark rock room: the location of my original nocturnal meeting with the Sidar.

Much like the tunnels in which we had originally met

the dwarfs, the ceiling of this room was low, appearing more so due to the height of the few standing Sidar. In the middle of the roof, an opening led upwards and I watched smoke from the central fire wander amidst the low light as it curled its way towards the heavens. It was ghostly in its path, flickering in the flames that lit the space.

Our two female guides spread out and sat down while Farzah joined an older Sidar, whom I recognized, on the other side of the room. He placed the torch he still carried in a bracket on the wall.

The older man approached me, hands extended with his palms up. I instinctively reached out for him and was not surprised when the mental connection sparked to life as we touched.

"*Thank you, Elon,*" he thought to me. I nodded and smiled. "*I am so glad you are here. And I am pleased that you have brought your friend.*"

With this, he broke our connection and reached out for Qidira. She moved toward him as well and they met halfway. He held her hands and smiled. I could not tell if they were communicating or not, but then he spoke and I figured they had just been looking at each other.

"Qidira . . . we meet again." He pulled her to his chest in a familiar embrace. After a few breaths, during which I gaped in confusion, he held her at arm's length. "It is delightful to see you."

I could not contain my surprise. "What?" My voice echoed around the cave, breaking the meditative silence that shrouded the space. It took me one stride to reach them and I leaned down into Qidira's face. "You've been here? You've met them, and you didn't tell me?"

Qidira's expression held a mixture of angst, anger, and sadness. "There is a lot I have not told you," she said finally, sorrow and apprehension in her voice. My indignation fizzled to nothing. This was not her style; she was more prone to righteous indignation, not servile self-reproach. This was just bizarre. "Amil made me promise never to tell anyone. And I did, Elon, I promised."

I understood. "Okay." Still, I eyed her suspiciously. "Anything else I should know?" I looked from her to Emir, and back again.

Qidira grasped my hands. "I, uh . . ." She looked at the older man then back to me. "I am sorry. I cannot tell you how hard it has been for me not to talk about it. I know you thought I was brooding when I pulled away, but I could not tell you what was going on. Trust me when I say that it tore me up." Releasing my hands, she pulled at a small part of her skirt and twisted it over and over.

A hand touched my shoulder at the same time as long, pale fingers rested on Qidira. I saw that my old Sidar friend was bridging the gap between us. He said, into my mind, *"You will know now, she can tell you whatever she wishes now that you are here, too."* I smiled and nodded, first at him, and then at Qidira. He continued, out loud, "Qidira, would you like to make the formal introductions?"

"Oh, uh, sure," she stammered. "Elon, this is Emir. This is Amil's father." She said the last part with a half-smile. Her eyebrows and shoulders rose in expectation of my surprise. And it came.

"What? Again, something you perhaps could have told me. Your father-in-law is—"

"The elder of the Sidar sect on Palus, yes," she said with an "oops aren't I cute" smile.

"Technically," Emir added jovially, "Amil is the succeeding prince, so that makes her, you," he said, turning to Qidira, "our princess."

"Oh," I said, laughing sardonically, "you are loving this. And I can only *imagine* what it took for you not to tell me *this* part." She just smiled and swished her skirts around. "A fairy princess. My best friend is a fairy princess. Great, I will never hear the end of this." Qidira closed the distance between us and wrapped her arms around my waist.

"I'm so glad that you love me already," she said, laughing.

"Yeah, watch yourself," I replied, hugging her back. To Emir I said, "It is an honor to formally meet you. I know that I am here for, well, a task, but before we get to that, I must ask, on behalf of my dear friend Qidira: where is Amil?"

Emir paused. "Ah yes, please sit down."

We joined the Sidar on the ground and Emir introduced the rest of the room. There were eight Sidar in total, and none of them looked Other.

Emir looked at Qidira. "Amil left us, a while ago, to live on the mountainside." Qidira's eyes widened and she looked to me for clarification.

I shrugged, my face clearly reminding her that I was the one with the least information among the three of us. To Emir, I said, "What does that mean?"

"He returned to us when you left—"

"I left?" Qidira exclaimed. Indignation and fury spilled from her flashing eyes.

"Yes, that is what he told us." Emir was visibly taken aback by her anger.

"*He* left *me*," she spat. "He left me, with our little baby boy, out on that ledge, in that cave on the mountainside." She gesticulated wildly in one direction, seemed to think about it, pointed in another, then gave up with a Qidira-huff. "I had to fight through the snow, across the face of the mountain, with my son strapped to my back to make it to the first settlement. It took me months to even be able to speak again, and he is saying *I* left *him?*" Her eyes swam with the power I had seen back in Truth and I felt it lick my skin like a flame.

"Stop, please," I said with fear. This seemed to interrupt her ire and she took her eyes off of Emir, calming the fire they held.

The older Sidar took advantage of her pause. "We often thought he was being untruthful; it is difficult to hide anything from one's sect. But we did not pry. I have long thought that it was whatever secret he was keeping from us that drove him away. He returned to the cave where you two lived; there is a connection with Truth through the tunnels that lead there."

Surprise flared on Qidira's face.

Emir continued, "So we still have contact with him. I go out there often and bring him supplies." I saw the father in Emir shining in his expression.

"He sits there," he continued, "looking over the edge at the marsh. He watches you." He said this last part quietly and paused, waiting for it to sink in.

"He . . . he has been watching me?" Qidira said softly. I put an arm around her shoulder.

Emir nodded. "Yes. And it has taken all he could muster to not invade Elon's mind in order to see through her eyes."

"Say what?" I said.

To me, Emir said, "We have the power to see through another Sidar's eyes, if allowed. And, with enough energy, usually almost enough that it would kill us, we can force our way into another's mind and use their eyes. It is forbidden, a high crime among the Sidar. But Amil told me that he has wanted to see Qidira again and for this, he was willing to die." He sighed.

"I have often wondered if he would even be able to

reach you given how strong the protection is around your house in the marsh. There is fairy magic at work there, this much we definitely know. We can never reach you, Elon, unless you are out of the house, physically or mentally." He saw the look on my face and clarified, "When you sleep your mind leaves the house sometimes, searching for . . . something. We like to think you are looking for us, and so we join you, giving you warmth and comfort. But we know there are other longings in your heart, and so we never push you."

"I . . . I appreciate that." I suddenly felt vulnerable and exposed. This whole time I had been open to mental attack while I slept and it was only the beneficence of the Sidar that kept me safe.

Fabulous, I thought, my own sarcasm resounding in my mind.

"And now, while I would love to continue to discuss my family, we have other, more pressing issues at hand. Elon, we would like to give you more information about why you are here, if you are ready to hear it."

"Sure, of course." I became aware once again of the others in the room.

Emir settled himself into his body, straightening his posture. He extended his hands toward me and I saw all of those around us close their eyes, their bodies becoming rigid. I reached out for him and the connection between us was once again established.

THE STAR

*a*s a collective, Emir and the other Sidar relayed the story of the Sidra, the Star. We began with the Sidar creation story and continued through to the arrival of the Sidar on Palus. The journey through history began with a verbal story in my mind but transformed into a wash of telepathic images from Emir's memory.

Sidra was the evolutionary home to the Sidar. Their creation story says that millions of years prior a star had fallen to the planet and created life. That star, the Sidra, possessed great power and energy, and when it fell into the swampy landscape of the planet the energy interacted with what was there and life sprang up. The planet was, therefore, named after its cosmic origin.

Evolution occurred, with empathy and telepathy being the means of communication. The location of the Star was naturally felt by all Sidar on the planet, and their society evolved and grew up around the deep resting place of this power source.

Approximately ten thousand years ago, the first ship carrying vamphyres and humans arrived. It was then that verbal communication made its debut in Sidar history. The original vamphyres were refugees from a planet where they were persecuted for sharing life and love with humans; they were welcomed on Sidra and the two cultures grew, for the most part, separately. The vamphyres' genetic need still necessitated occasional human sacrifice and the Sidar were fundamentally opposed to killing. Still, both societies grew richly, with music and art, and their own justice systems.

Originally, the Sidar had no need for punishment, as they were a communal people with no secrets from anyone. In turn, the vamphyres policed themselves. Sidar telepathy was stronger than the vamphyres. The vamphyres could sense power, could somehow pinpoint an individual with empathic ability, however, their power lacked the ability to *read* another's mind. Their strength lay in their ability to *control* it.

The more the two cultures interacted, the more Other were born on the planet. Individuals who had both the power of telepathy and the power of mind control grew up amidst the increasingly more confusing backdrop of mixed cultures. Genetic drift also created children with barriers against both of these powers, making internal policing ineffective. Societal norms were broken, respect of life became threatened, and rogue sects of both vamphyres and Sidar broke off and created their own compounds.

Soon, rogue vamphyres began feeding on the limited pure human population. The two societies were faced with a problem: how to manage the deviant vamphyres. For a while, Other were placed in charge of hunting down and disposing of the wrong-doers, and there were complaints of discrimination, and of genocide, against the Sidar.

An Empathic Council was created, and Council members were granted the right to use their abilities to detect deceit and wrong-doings. It was equally seated with

Sidar, vamphyres, and Other. The council worked well for a while—the Sidar detecting infractions and the vamphyres bringing in the offenders. But the vamphyres started to distrust the Sidar; they resented the Sidar's ability to know what was going on around the planet.

One day a vamphyric council member, Vladimir, who had been quietly raising a following, stormed into the main council building and killed the other members of the council, vamphyre and Sidar alike. He and his people killed and fed on them all—except for one.

Throughout Sidar history, there had been one individual who was charged with the care of the Sidra. This person was known as the Custodier. The Custodier lived near the Star, keeping his or her psychic connection to the power source; only the Custodier was told the exact location of the pieces. This was a holy position, granted to a new child when the old Custodier was nearing death. The chosen individual lived a life of solitude, prayer, and introspection. The Custodier was a conduit for the power of the Star.

It was this Custodier who was spared; her name was Azita. Vladimir demanded that she take him to the Sidra. She refused and Vladimir and his men brutalized and fed upon her until she was near death.

Still, she refused to reveal the location of the Star.

Vladimir pulled down the temple stone by stone; he dug a hole as deep as he could. He was obsessed with finding the Sidra and using its power to create dominance for the vamphyre population.

His obsession drove him for years, and he kept Azita close to death the entire time, chained to the wall in his living quarters. He fed on her and used his powers to attempt to force her into revealing the location of the Star.

But Azita, fortified by her connection to the Sidra, was stronger than he was, and he was unsuccessful.

One moonless night, during a seasonal lighting storm, Azita quietly choked out the words, "I am ready."

Vladimir unchained her and she led him outside, to the side of the seemingly bottomless hole he had created in an attempt to find the Sidra. She raised her arms and was struck simultaneously by two bolts of lightning. Her clothes, hair, and flesh caught on fire. She ran to Vladimir and, embracing him, threw herself into the pit, taking him with her. Neither of them was ever seen again.

The next morning, a Sidar girl child appeared at the side of the chasm. With the chaos surrounding the disappearance of Vladimir and his captive, the child was ignored, and no one noticed when she disappeared over the edge. No one noticed as she wound her way down ladders, and across bridges, past watch stations and mining tunnels along the way. No one noticed that the deeper she got, the more the rock glowed when she was near it, and no one noticed when she slipped through a fissure in the stone that only a child could fit through.

That night the lightning continued and, with their leader missing, none of the now ruling rebel vamphyres took the time to notice the unusual amount of lightning striking deep in the chasm. Those that did see it were the Sidar that were working down in the dark mines. They saw the lightning; they saw it go through the small fracture in the rock. They alone felt the new pull into the earth and they followed it.

The small girl child called to them. Sitting in front of the Sidra, deep in the earth, she reached out carefully to the pure Sidar on the planet and told them who she was— the new Custodier. Some were afraid to go to her, and those that did risk the trip were killed along the way by vamphyre rebels for being out at night.

As the lightning subsided, and dawn was near, a light began to shine up from the bottom of the chasm. As it grew brighter, a warm wind rose out of the gaping hole. A noise like a cyclone pulsed, and soon, out of the wide gap in the earth, rose the Sidra, the center stone shining like a star with its three satellites whirling in their blurred interwoven orbits. Sitting on the center sphere was the girl. She expanded her mind and, in an instant, found every vamphyre that was anywhere nearby. She threw out her arms and the peripheral satellites whirled off with great speed, and killed everyone with vamphyre blood within a five thousand click radius.

The child lowered the Sidra down to the earth next to a group of waiting Sidar. She wordlessly touched three of them and the three missing spheres rushed back to the chosen individuals. She raised her hands to the sky, and, calling on every Sidar on the planet, opened up a powerful vortex into which she, and any nearby, willing Sidar, were ferociously drawn. The sky closed behind them and stillness settled over the planet, a stillness which had not been there in thousands of years.

Most of Vladimir's followers perished that day, along with some innocents. Not all of those responsible for the atrocities against the Sidar died, however. Some vamphyres, living in compounds scattered across the countryside, survived. It was these vamphyres that rallied and, racing against the rising sun, made it to their waiting ships. One of these ships, using the force of the vortex, followed the Sidar through and off into space.

The next part of the story was similar to that which was told by the dwarfs: the lights in the sky, the arrival of the Sidar into Truth, and their request for asylum; the invasion of the vamphyres and the killings of the dwarfs and Other; and the sequestration of the Sidar deep into the mountains.

Emir explained how the Sidar compound was created. The Sidra itself shaped the smooth passageways through which we had traveled, infusing them with the power to repel enemies. It then built the city of Laet and supplied the dwarfs with caverns full of eternal food and fresh water. I was treated to images in my mind as seen by Emir in his childhood, of the dwarf habitat and of life on Palus for the remaining Sidar.

"I am a distant cousin to the girl child who saved the Sidar. I am the current Custodier," Emir said aloud when the tale reached its end.

I shook my head, blinking as my eyes re-acclimated to the dimness of the cave. With the memory of the Star's brilliance fresh in my mind, I looked around for some indication of where the Sidra might be.

"You will not see it," Emir said, "but you will feel it if you are still."

I did not think I had it in me to be quiet any longer. "So, what do you want from me? What can I do in all of this?"

"On arrival to this planet, we as a people decided it was better to split the Star apart for fear of it being found by the wrong people. We need you to find these parts of the Sidra." He stared at me, unblinking. "Wait, you can't remember where you put them? Like, you lost them?" Doubt shone on my face. "Didn't you just say you could feel it? You must know where the other parts are."

He laughed. "It is not that we cannot remember where the separate parts were placed, it is just that"—he paused — "two of them have become obfuscated."

"Who hid them?" Qidira chimed in.

Emir turned to her and said, "My brother took one. The others were given to Sidar who never returned."

"And you can't sense them? What about the main part of the Sidra, can't that re-call them or something?" I asked.

"It is true that the heart of the Star has power over its satellites, but they must be within a certain distance of each other, and not be obscured by other magic."

Ahh, I thought, *there's the problem.* "So, these parts are somewhere where there is other magic."

"Two of them are, yes." He frowned. "One of them is in a cave, miles away on the other side of the mountains, where the rock falls into the water. It is surrounded by magic that blocks it from us, too, but we know that it is there."

"Can't *you* go get it?" I asked, more out of belligerence than unwillingness.

"We could, but we prefer not to leave here, especially now with these new invaders. Shirah goes out because she is mostly human. Those of us who are full blooded Sidar prefer to keep protected under the energy field. Imagine what would happen if all of a sudden there was a psychic blip on the vamphyre radar anywhere near where we are? They would know where to look."

"What about Amil?" Qidira asked. "Isn't he vulnerable out there in the cave? Doesn't he show up to the vamphyres?"

"Are you forgetting your protection spell?" Emir asked, smiling.

Qidira looked taken aback. "I left no spell."

"You did. You prayed before you left, and little did you know that your prayers cast a fairy spell. You prayed to keep Amil safe from harm, and that is what you have done. His powers are shielded from the vamphyres below."

Qidira considered the floor quietly.

"Okay, so here I am." I paused before asking my next question. "But why me?" I bit back any further questions, realizing that their whole population was facing possible annihilation and assuaging my self-doubt was minor in light of their current situation. "I'm sorry," I quickly apologized, "I guess it doesn't matter."

"Oh, but it does matter," Emir replied. He put a finger under my chin and raised my eyes to his. "It has everything to do with your parents, and where you were born."

The mention of my parents made my stomach flip and I thought about what he had said. I was born on Sidra, but other than that . . . my parents only said we left so that I could have a better life. I knew nothing of the situation surrounding my birth.

He continued, "You will know, in good time."

That just annoyed me, and I am sure my face registered as much because Emir released a chuckle reserved for younger generations who are in a hurry to learn the meaning of life too soon.

"Yeah, well," I said, "whatever." I drew in a long, deep breath, to gather myself and attempt to curb my annoyance. After releasing my breath slowly through pursed lips, I said, "So, where do we start?"

UNDER SIEGE

*B*efore Emir was able to answer my question, searing pain tore through my psyche. It struck me at the same time as the rest of the Sidar around me: pain, fear, loss. In unison, the silent Sidar gasped.

Emir jumped to his feet and telepathically relayed directions to the collective. *"Quickly, into the caves."*

In a flurry of white robes and wild, blond hair, the Sidar in the room evacuated via an almost unseen crevasse on the wall opposite where we entered.

"What's going on?" Qidira implored. She, too, was on her feet, but obviously she had not heard Emir's instructions. Nor, I realized, had she felt the pain and angst.

I moved to stand next to her. "Something horrible is happening, I felt it. Then Emir directed them all to leave, to go into 'the caves'."

I gazed in the direction from which the pangs of fear and pain radiated. Screams echoed in my head and heart. Without thinking, I started back toward Laet, toward the melee now ringing throughout my entire body.

Before he, too, fled, Emir grabbed my arm. "No, Elon,

you must not go. We have to hide. We cannot save them now."

"You're kidding, right?"

Qidira, exasperated with her lack of information, stomped a foot. "What is happening? Who can't we save?"

I looked into her eyes. "There are vamps in Laet."

Together, Emir and I cringed. Every hit in Laet, every death, bit at our psyche. Blow after blow fell in the city and each death tore at our souls.

"Qid, I have to help them."

"You can't," Emir asserted.

"You obviously don't understand who you're talking to," Qidira said. "Elon, come on." She took hold of my hand and pulled me toward the exit.

Ignoring Emir's continued pleadings for me to remain with them, Qidira continued pulling me toward the tunnel leading to Laet.

Before we left the room, I grasped her shoulders. "I need you to stay here."

She looked at me with confusion and belligerence. "Why would I do that?"

"You are not a fighter. As it is, I'll likely be woefully outnumbered."

"But—"

Frustration filled my words when I spoke. "Will you listen to me, for once in your life?" I stepped backwards into the tunnel opening. I grabbed a torch from the wall and then, pointing a long finger at her, I commanded, "Stay here."

I spun on my toes and rushed toward the falling Sidar city. No sooner had I gone a few clicks then I heard Qidira's footfalls behind me. I did not have time to argue with her, so I continued my dash towards the massacre. Turn after turn, I hurried through the rough tunnel, moving closer to the chaos with every step. The psychic stabs of death became less frequent, and while grateful for relief, the next time I felt a Sidar die, it was that much more devastating.

Cursing my inability to go faster, I hurtled forward. Eventually, I found myself, once again, faced with a solid, stone wall.

"*No!*" My cry echoed through the dark space. "No, no, no." I pounded the rock with my free hand.

Stepping back, I handed to the torch to Qidira and drew my sword. Qidira stopped my hand as I pulled the weapon over my head in preparation to strike the barrier.

"It is stone and it is magic." Her breath came in spurts as she struggled to recover from the effort of keeping up with my sprint. "Not even a dwarf sword can penetrate it."

"You're a fairy, can't you do something?"

She looked astounded. "This is Sidar magic, Elon. Nothing I know how to do would work. Besides, this is your arena."

Realizing she was right, I sheathed my sword and stepped up to the smooth stone. I pressed my whole body against it, as I had done to the ship in the marsh. The rock, cold against my cheek, felt more forgiving, however, than the metal had and my mind easily passed through the wall.

Stronger now than before, my energy sailed through open space until I found myself in the halls under the city. This time, I had vision as well. It was not like seeing with my eyes but still an image of the surroundings grew in my mind's eye.

All screaming had stopped and the silence scared me more than any noise could. I crept up the stairs into the courtyard. No breeze ruffled my energy. No sunlight met my careful examination. Instead, everything was dark. Snow showered down from the sky and blanketed every surface. Cold permeated my mind and I soon realized it was not just from the temperature.

I pulled back and tried to remain small. Dark figures zipped through the air, in and out of balcony openings. Bodies littered the ground, partially obscured by the gathering snow. Still, as flakes fell onto patches of open wounds, the fluffy material melted against hot blood and splotches of red dotted the bleak landscape like a child's macabre painting.

Attempting to remain undetected just below the courtyard surface, I felt something approach and knew I had failed in my endeavor to hide. The oily presence slunk along the ground, slithering like a spectral serpent in its path toward me. It did not rush; it did not slam into me and accost my senses. Soon, it simply slid to a stop and hovered near me.

"There you are. Why must we keep chasing you? Come join us and no one else needs to be hurt. I thought for sure my present for you in the village would convince you of our power." This energy, this slimy female, sensed my rage as images of Strom's mutilated body filled my mind. A hollow chuckle echoed in my head. *"Think about it. We'll be waiting . . ."*

In a whorl of red, gray, and white, I zoomed back to my body. With a crash, I found myself on the ground of the tunnel, panting.

"Elon." Qidira dropped to my side. "What happened?"

I closed my eyes and let my head drop to the cold stone. "They're here, Qid. The vamps from the ship in the marsh killed every Sidar in Laet."

Qidira clamped a hand over her mouth. Her head moved slowly back and forth as tears cascaded down her cheeks.

I opened my eyes and stared at the stone ceiling. "I

don't know what to do. They're looking for me. She said they're looking for me."

"She?"

"I have to go to them." I got to my feet. Straightening my sword and checking for Morningstar, I started back toward the cave where we met Emir.

Qidira grasped my arm as I went and spun me around. "What 'she,' Elon?"

I sputtered, not sure how to explain. "Some female vamp." I thought back to the malevolent presence I encountered in the marsh and knew I had, once again, experienced the cold psyche of the pure vamphyre who struck fear into the hearts of even her own crew. To Qidira I continued, "She's strong, stronger than I've ever experienced. She knew me. Somehow, she knew me." Qidira dropped her hold on me and I looked around the small space as if a sign might appear directing me what to do next. When none came, I said, "If I don't go, more people will die. I have to see what she wants from me." Again, I turned to find a way back to the marsh.

"Don't be an idiot," Qidira spat.

I spun on my heels. "What?" While disagreements were not new to us, name calling had never been a part of our discourse. I was unsure how to respond.

Qidira closed the space between us and, reaching up to clasp my face in her hands, stared into my eyes. "Do you really think it is going to be that easy? You cannot go to them, Elon. The Sidar and the dwarfs have all said that it is you who needs to face this thing. You cannot give in and give them what they want, which, apparently, is you."

I pulled away and paced the small space. Hands on my hips, I said, "Why didn't they just take me out in the marsh then? I was alone, unprotected, and plastered against their ship? I mean, I all but threw myself at them." I huffed and then mumbled under my breath, "Freaking brilliant, Elon. 'Oh, let me go see what's in this huge ship, alone. While I'm at it, I'll try to become one with this alien craft.' You're right," I addressed Qidira, "I am an idiot."

Qidira's face screwed into a mask of concern. "You are not an idiot. I said don't *be* an idiot, not that you *are* an idiot." Again, she attempted to comfort me. Taking my hands in hers she said, "Take a deep breath."

She demonstrated the action. I released a sardonic grumble but followed her direction anyway.

Qidira continued. "My guess? They want you *and* the Star."

"Well, I don't have the Star, and I sure won't give it to them once I find it."

"So now you're going to find it? A moment ago, you were ready to give in and go to them."

I glared at her and returned to pacing the space. As I walked the same path over and over again, I wrestled with continued indecision. I needed to protect the Sidar that were left. If the invaders wanted me, then why not go to them and take my chances? Once they had me though, what would they do? If they really wanted the Star, they would do to me what they had done all those years ago to Azita: captivity and torture. Surety solidified in my gut. "I can't let them get the Star."

"No, you can't."

She was right. She was almost always right. I, on the other hand, was emotional and prone to decisions based on impulse. None of this insight soothed my growing sense of dread, however; my brain continued to lead me to the same conclusion: in order to protect the Sidar, the dwarfs, and the humans, for that matter, the easiest thing to do was go to this dark adversary.

Easiest for me, at least.

Like a flash of undeserved celestial blessing, my father's voice echoed in my brain. *"Choose wisely, Hoshi. Do not underestimate yourself, or your enemy. You can choose to serve yourself or you can be of service to the universe. Choose wisely."*

Embrace your power

ACKNOWLEDGMENTS

My deepest thanks to all who listened to my many musings during the evolution of Elon's story. You know who you are.

For Qidira, who inspired me to continue learning more about Elon and her world. Every time you read a new installment, your response was always, "More." Your faith in me is irreplaceable.

For Fella, who read, and re-read, every permutation. I can't imagine how confusing that must have been.

Thank you to Sarina, who endlessly reviewed my changes; Ignacia, who offered long-distance smiles- I knew you were there, even when we did not speak; and Aadnon & Malachy...even though your upset boiled near the top, you stood by my side every day.

An undying thank-you must be given to artist Anna Carley for her amazing inside art (for more from Anna, please see https://elonthebook.com/art-by-anna-carley).

And finally, thank you to all warriors out there who struggle to embrace their power. Keep up the good fight.

ABOUT THE AUTHOR

Isabella Adams is an emerging author whose release of *Elon* takes her across genre borders. Having debuted into the world of mystery and detective fiction with her novel *Last Man Out*, Isabella now dances across the fantasy border with *Elon*.

Isabella lives and works on the Gulf Coast of Florida as a Family Medicine physician. As most of her stories do, *Elon* began as a dream. This one, however, occurred during daylight hours, while Isabella slept after a long night shift in the ICU. Once awake, Isabella scurried to write down the dream. Having to stop writing in order to return to the hospital, Isabella was nonetheless compelled to complete the tale. One paragraph or sentence at a time, *Elon* made its way onto paper.

Once one long manuscript, *Elon* now exists as a trilogy. The second installment, *The Custodier*, continues the friends' journey through Palus while the third novel, *Battle For The Star*, culminates in a final show-down for dominance of The Sidra. Stay tuned for more adventures with Elon and Qidira.

www.izzyadams.com